TOO MANY PO

'By the time you get t...
This really is the holi...
Aunt, Sue. P.S. I haven't a care in the world
knowing the ponies are in such good hands.'

Far away from her home, the aunt of
Pippa's new friend Jane has no idea that life
on her West Country pony farm isn't
running at all smoothly.

When the stable lad leaves for a new job,
Pippa offers to help out on the farm. It
seems the ideal way to spend a summer
holiday – there are plenty of ponies to care
for and even room for her own beloved
Magic.

Then some unexpected visitors arrive,
together with even *more* ponies. They seem
well-intentioned and helpful – especially
when Magic gets colic – but Pippa has an
uneasy feeling about them. Is it just
coincidence that sheep and pony rustlers
are operating in the area? Pippa becomes
more and more convinced that the ponies
on the farm are in danger, but how can she
prove her suspicions are well founded?

The fourth book in the Pippa Pony series

Too Many Ponies for Pippa

Judith M. Berrisford

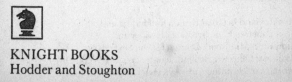

KNIGHT BOOKS
Hodder and Stoughton

For Joanna and Peter Yates, remembering happy times with their wonderful grandparents, Gordon and Cynthia Dudley

Copyright © 1984 Judith M. Berrisford
First published by Knight Books 1984

British Library C.I.P.

Berrisford, Judith M.
   Too many ponies for Pippa
   I. Title
   823'.914[F]   PZ7

ISBN 0 340 32092 3

Printed and bound in Great Britain for Hodder and Stoughton Paperbacks, a division of Hodder and Stoughton Ltd., Mill Road, Dunton Green, Sevenoaks, Kent (Editorial Office: 47 Bedford Square, London, WC1 3DP) by Hunt Barnard Printing Ltd., Aylesbury, Bucks.

Contents

1

An unexpected meeting

'This way, Magic!'

Pulling on my right rein and with my left leg near to my pony's side to prevent her quarters swinging out, I tried to turn my Welsh-Arabian in the direction of Abbot's Coombe.

However, my usually obedient pony had decided that she wanted to take another route. She circled obstinately, pointing her head towards a deep lane that led to the moors.

'Come on, Magic! We're late already. Pete and Dave will be wondering what's happened to us.'

We were on our way to join my twin brother and his best friend, farmer's son Dave. The boys had taken the sheepdog, Glen, and were camping out in an orchard belonging to an old friend of Dave's mother, so as to be near the sheepdog trials.

Dave had been training Glen for weeks and was hoping to win a good place in the trials.

I was being allowed to join them, with my pony Magic, on condition that I stayed over the village shop with Dave's mother's friend.

'Don't be so wilful, Magic,' I scolded as my pony

edged again towards the lane.

I touched her with my stick but Magic dug in her toes. Poking her nose forward she took a determined step towards the lane.

'I can't think what's got into you,' I groaned, sliding to the ground and grasping her rein near the bit. 'Well, I haven't time to waste arguing.'

I led her firmly on to the Abbot's Coombe road.

At that moment pony-noises sounded from around the bend in the lane. There was a shrill whinny, followed by the sound of cantering hooves.

Magic cocked an ear in the direction of the hoof-beats and tried to pull back into the lane. I hesitated, wondering what pony upset was taking place.

Magic spun round, snatched the reins from my grasp and trotted towards the clattering hooves. I ran after her, caught a foot on a stone and tripped over.

'Come back!' I scolded. 'Oh, you bad pony!'

Then round the bend came a jostling, mealy-nosed mass – seven Exmoor ponies and a leggy foal.

'Stop them!' called a despairing voice from behind the ponies.

I caught a glimpse of a chestnut-haired girl of about sixteen. Then Magic and the pony stampede met and became a confused muddle of squealing ponies.

From my side of the pony mix-up I grabbed

Magic; then held one of the Exmoors by the forelock. The girl caught two more of the ponies. From the shifting mass of rounded bodies, neat heads and milling hooves emerged a curly-haired small boy.

'The cause of all the trouble!' groaned the girl. 'My young brother, Darren! I'd better introduce myself. I'm Jane Holt.'

'And I'm Pippa Woodley.'

Darren reached up to put podgy arms around the neck of the foal.

'Darren let the ponies out of the field,' Jane explained. 'I told him to wait for me before he opened the gate but he was in a hurry.'

'I wanted to go to the shop for an iced lolly,' piped Darren. 'I thought I could get through the gate without the ponies following. But I couldn't.'

'Too right he couldn't,' sighed his sister. 'Now I've got to try and get the mares back . . . somehow.' She turned to the boy. 'You'll be too late for your iced lolly, Darren. Perhaps that'll teach you to do what you're told.'

'Let me help you drive the ponies,' I offered, putting my foot into Magic's stirrup and swinging myself into the saddle. 'I'm on my way to the Abbot's Coombe shop. Maybe we can all go together later.'

'And all have iced lollies!' The girl gave a friendly smile and turned to lead back up the lane the two ponies she was holding.

With Darren spreading out his arms by my side,

9

we persuaded the other mares to follow. The foal walked happily beside his mother.

When we rounded the bend Jane suddenly stopped in surprise as she saw a slim, fair-haired boy, of about seventeen, who was walking towards us. He was wearing cord trousers with a blue body-warmer over a white roll-top sweater and he had a suitcase in his hand.

'Micky!' Jane gasped as the foal frolicked towards him. 'Where do you think you're going?'

'That's what I was coming to tell you.' The boy turned to fend off the foal who was pushing its muzzle against his chest. 'Hey, Dandy! Keep off! That's my best sweater you're wiping your mouth on.'

'But what's happened?' Jane persisted. 'Why are you all dressed up?'

'I've got a new job.' Micky dropped his gaze. 'At a racing stable near Dunster. I didn't know how to tell you. In fact I hoped I wasn't going to have to say anything about it before your Auntie Sue got back. But I'm needed in a hurry. One of their stable lads has broken his collar-bone. They're short-handed.'

'So are we.' Jane stared at him in dismay. 'You can't got off like this, Micky . . . Your mother's gone to look after her sister and can't help out here. Auntie Sue won't be back from her cruise for another fortnight. How do you think I'm to manage?'

'That's what's been worrying me.' Micky

shifted his feet; then he looked more fully at me. 'But now it seems as though you've found a new pony pal to help you.'

'I don't know about that,' I said, not sure what Jane would feel about such a solution. 'I'm supposed to be going to stay in Abbot's Coombe. My brother Pete and his friend Dave Garland have entered a dog in the Young Farmers' Class of the Sheepdog Trials. Mrs Farley who keeps the Corner Shop in Abbot's Coombe was at school with Dave's mum. I'm to stay with her, and the boys are camping in her orchard.'

'There you are then,' said Micky. 'If your brother and his pal are busy with their dog, you and your pony'll be at a loose end. You'd be better off staying here with Jane.'

'Do you think you could?' Jane turned to me hopefully. 'Another pony girl! Between us we ought to manage.'

'To be honest, I don't know a lot about ponies.' I patted my pony's neck. 'I've had Magic for only a few months. Before that I just used to help out at the local stables.'

'You'll do,' Micky encouraged. 'There are only seven mares and the foal here. You'll find it a piece of cake.' He glanced at his watch. 'Well, girls, it's a quarter-past-three. I'll have to go or I'll miss the bus into Dunster. Very sorry!'

'Wait a minute,' said Jane. 'You haven't told us yet where you're going. Where shall we send your mail?'

'Downham Stables, Dunster.' Micky's eyes lit up. 'It's a training establishment – a real step up in the horse world. I shall be looking after racehorses. I'll be able to ride gallops. If I please the bosses I might even get an apprenticeship as a jockey.'

'I suppose I'd better wish you luck, then, Micky,' Jane said sadly. 'That's how Auntie Sue would want it. She wouldn't want to stand in the way of your getting on in the horse world.'

She held out her hand and Micky took it. 'I'll be in touch, Jane.'

We watched Micky walking away. At the bend he turned to wave. Then he was out of sight.

Jane looked forlornly down the empty lane. Then she turned to the ponies who were now cropping the verge.

'The ponies are going to miss Micky. So am I. He's the best stable lad ever.' She looked at me desperately. 'Is there any hope that you might be able to help, Pippa? You could stay in the house with Darren and me. You're pony-mad, like me. So it wouldn't seem a chore. We could have fun. Oh, do say "yes".'

2

Noises in the night

'But we need you here,' my twin Pete insisted.

'Yes, the idea was for you to stay in Mrs Farley's spare room above the shop,' Dave added, 'and to put Magic in the field while Pete, Glen and I camp in the orchard.'

I sighed.

'Oh, you don't understand. I can't let Jane down. Her aunt won this fabulous cruise. The organisers wouldn't let her have the money instead. So she had to go. It was a chance she couldn't miss; only now her daily-help has gone to stay with a sick sister and the daily's son, Micky, who was the stable lad, has found a better job. Jane's in trouble because she's all on her own with seven ponies and a foal to look after as well as her young brother to keep an eye on.'

'I can understand that, Pippa.' Dave's good-natured face showed his concern. 'You're torn between two loyalties. But I think you ought to remember that you've only just met Jane while my mother and Mrs Farley were school friends. Mum only suggested your coming with us because she thought your company would do Mrs Farley good. Mrs Farley was widowed last year and since then she's had a burglary. She needs someone to take her out of herself.'

'She'll have you and Pete,' I countered.

'Yes, but we'll be camping in the orchard,' said Dave, 'and anyway we'll be too busy with Glen to spend much time with Mrs Farley.'

'Come on, Pippa,' Pete coaxed. 'You know you're wanted here.'

'Oh, don't go on!' I was exasperated. 'You and Dave made it plain that you didn't want me and Magic around during the trials. You kept on saying that I might upset Glen and stop him keeping his mind on the sheep.'

'So you used to, fussing him all the time.' Pete put his hand on my shoulder. 'But I think you've learnt your lesson now, twin.'

'Oh, don't be so patronising! Just because I've found something better to do than tamely watch you and Dave put Glen through his paces.'

'Be reasonable, Pippa, and face facts.' Pete seemed to be losing his patience. 'Who's going to do the cooking if you're not around?'

'Charming!' I retorted. 'So that's why you suddenly decide you want me. Pity you didn't join the scouts and do a bit of camp cookery instead of spending all your time on football, athletics and now sheepdogs. Yes, it was super when you got interested in ponies and we went pony-trekking and when we were at Stableways. But since we came to live in Somerset you've spent most of your time with Dave; and I've felt the odd one out. Now I've made a real pony friend of my own, you're trying to spoil things.'

Pete kicked at a tuft of grass, then side-stepped as Magic tried to nibble his shoulder. 'Pity I didn't have a boy twin,' he growled.

I was about to take a swing at him with Magic's hay-net when Dave cut in.

'Pippa! Pete! Be your age! Come on! I need *both* of you to lend a hand with the tent guy-ropes.'

Just then the back door of the village shop was flung open and Mrs Farley's face appeared. Her voice floated over the currant bushes.

'Are you there, Pippa? Oh, thank goodness! Come and serve in the shop, dear, while I cope with a traveller.'

Pete touched my arm and gave a winning smile.

'There you are, Pippa! Everybody needs you!'

* * * *

I telephoned my new friend after tea.

'So you see, Jane, I can't come and sleep at the Pony Farm tonight,' I told her, 'and tomorrow I'll have to cook the boys' breakfast and teach them how to fry eggs and bacon on a primus.'

'They sound a helpless pair,' Jane commented.

'Not really,' I said. 'After I've taught them some simple cooking I think they'll be able to manage.'

'So you'll be along later?' Jane's tone was almost

pleading but before I could reply, she gave a sudden shriek and, over the phone, I heard a clatter and a bang.

'Just a minute, Pippa.' Jane sounded bothered. 'Panic-stations! I forgot to shut the door when I answered the phone and Strawberry's followed me into the kitchen . . . Oh, you bad pony! No! You mustn't chew the telephone wires.' I heard a slap and the sound of pony hooves on a quarry floor followed by the slam of a door.

'Sorry, Pippa,' Jane said breathlessly. 'It's all go, what with Darren and the ponies and being single-handed now that Micky's walked out.'

I sighed. 'Oh, Jane, I feel I've let you down. But somehow or other I'll get over tomorrow to help.'

'Terrific, Pippa. You're a pal.'

* * * *

Despite being in a strange bed I soon fell asleep in the little bedroom over the shop. I was too tired to dream even about ponies.

I had snuggled down while it was still daylight but it seemed only the next moment that I was wide awake in the darkness and somebody was shaking my shoulder. There was a click and the beam of a torch and I blinked. My mouth felt dry.

'Who's that?' I gasped, sitting upright.

'It's only me,' Mrs Farley whispered tensely.

To reassure me, she turned the torch on herself and I saw that the pretty features, framed by her

16

wavy auburn hair, could scarcely hide a trace of fear.

'What's wrong?' I asked.

'Ssh! Don't make a noise,' Mrs Farley cautioned, 'and try not to be frightened, Pippa. I had to wake you. I think I've got burglars again. I woke with a start and now I'm not sure whether I heard anything or not. But something must have awakened me. Did you hear anything?'

'No, I was sound asleep,' I said. 'Perhaps you've had a bad dream. Let me make you a cup of tea.'

'Oh, don't go downstairs.' Mrs Farley tried to steady her voice. 'You might be attacked. I was last time. I'd heard breaking glass. Then a thud as someone jumped into the shop. I went down there and someone struck me. I didn't see them. I was badly bruised – it might have been worse . . . As it is, it's left me a bit jumpy even though I'm not really the nervy type. Sometimes I feel a bit ashamed of my fears . . . looking over my shoulder, flinching at shadows. Silly, isn't it?'

'No,' I said definitely. 'It's only natural after what you've been through.'

'Shush!' Mrs Farley suddenly interrupted. 'What was that?'

'I didn't hear anything . . .' I broke off as I heard a loud thud from outside the window and the sound of tinkling glass.

'It sounds as if they're getting in from the other side this time!' whispered Mrs Farley. 'I wonder if the boys are in danger out there in that tent?'

I scrambled out of bed and shut the bedroom door. 'Put out the torch, Mrs Farley. I'm going to pull back the curtain and look out.'

I crouched to the side of the window frame and tweaked the curtain. Then I heard running footsteps on the gravel path and two young male voices.

'Pippa!' came Dave's voice.

'Mrs Farley!' yelled Pete. 'Are you all right? Someone's been prowling about. He's tripped over the guy-ropes.'

'We'd better get the police.' Dave's voice floated out of the darkness. 'Dial 999.'

'We can't,' I shouted. 'The phone's in the shop and that's where the burglars are.' I turned to Mrs Farley. 'Let's all shout at once. Perhaps that will scare the thieves and make them run off.'

I stamped on the bedroom floor and shouted: 'Police! Get the police. Help! Help!'

'POLICE! POLICE!' called Mrs Farley, and the boys joined in below the window.

Then, as we all paused for breath, there came a whinny and I thought that perhaps the intruders weren't burglars this time. Perhaps they were pony thieves. Oh dear, they might be trying to steal Magic!

'Be off with you,' I shouted to the thieves. 'I won't let you take my pony.'

I ran down the stairs. Then, as I flung open the back door, my twin's voice sounded suddenly reassuring.

'Cool it, Pippa!'

'Panic's over!' added Dave. 'We've caught your so-called burglar.'

'Yes, it's that stupid pony of yours!' growled Pete. 'Now she's trodden on my toe and she won't let me catch her. Oh, come and cope, Pippa.'

'Magic!' I scolded.

Bare-footed, in my pyjamas, I sped over the dew-wet grass of the lawn to where my pony stood amid the blackcurrant bushes.

As I ran towards her, Magic moved away skittishly. Evidently she thought this was a grand game. She had now recovered from her fright and was enjoying all the fuss and commotion. She certainly didn't want to be caught and put back into her lonely field.

'You naughty pony!' I edged forward more cautiously now. If only I'd got a tit-bit to tempt her, but I hadn't and Magic dodged away again, trampling Mrs Farley's rhubarb.

'Look out, Pippa.' Pete moved through the raspberry canes to out-flank her. 'She's already damaged half the strawberry bed. There'll be nothing left of Mrs Farley's fruit if this goes on.'

'And I was counting on selling the strawberries and redcurrants in the shop,' Mrs Farley groaned. 'But, oh, what does that matter? At least we haven't had another break-in.'

There came a tinkle of broken glass as Magic backed into the garden frame.

'She's wrecking the place,' said Dave and bent

to unleash the sheepdog. 'Bring her in, Glen.'

The sheepdog dashed round the delphiniums to crouch in front of Magic. Dave gave two short whistles and Glen moved forward again.

Magic, noticing the dog, gave a playful toss of her head and trotted towards him.

Glen crouched again. He stared hard at Magic as if daring her to defy him, but Magic was no sheep, instinctively accustomed to obey a dog. She knew Glen as a friend who had sometimes joined in her games and accompanied us when we went for rides over the moors. Lowering her head, she walked towards Glen as if to blow at him affectionately.

Dave gave a long, high whistle.

The sheepdog's ears pricked. He rose and, with a swift, out-flanking movement, ran behind Magic, snapped at her heels and chivvied her through the open gateway into the field.

'See, Mrs Farley,' Pete said as he shut Magic inside, 'Glen's a first-class working dog.'

'And Magic's a thoroughly naughty pony,' Dave added. 'She's been here only a few hours and yet she's learnt to undo the gate of the field.'

'You don't know for sure that she did undo it,' I protested. 'There might have been a gap in the hedge.'

''Fraid not, Pippa,' Dave said. 'I checked the hedge last night. Look!'

In the moonlight he pointed to the field where Magic was already back at the gate.

'She's lonely!' Mrs Farley exclaimed. 'That's what she's trying to tell us. Perhaps she would be happier at the Pony Farm with the Exmoors.'

I smiled and suddenly felt hopeful.

'You'd have to go with her, of course, Pippa,' said Dave.

'I think so too,' nodded Mrs Farley.

'Definitely,' added Pete. 'Magic might be better behaved if she's with other ponies.'

'Yes, you've got to consider Magic,' Dave said and his eyes seemed to twinkle as though he was having a joke with me. 'The pony comes first. Ask any pony girl.'

'Oh, do you think so?' I looked at them all fondly. 'Thanks. I think you're being jolly good sports.'

3

More pony panic

'Now let me unload your kit, Pippa.' Jane put a hand on Magic's bridle. 'Then you can decide whether to put your pony with the others or in the Little Paddock by herself.'

'Well,' I reasoned, 'if she's with company she'll be less likely to try to get out.'

'Fair enough.' Jane glanced to the shady field where seven mealy-nosed Exmoor heads were crowding inquiringly round the gate while the long-legged foal flicked his still-short tail to keep the flies away.

'Unstrap your saddle-bags. Then we'll take off Magic's saddle and bridle and turn her into the field.' She moved towards an out-building beside the farmhouse. 'I'll fetch a head-collar so that we can catch her in case of trouble.'

While Jane and I were busy with Magic, Darren left the kitten he had been playing with and came to 'help'.

'I'll carry one of those for you, Pippa.' He tugged at the strap of one of the laden saddle-bags. 'I can manage it. See.'

He tried to pick up the saddle-bag by the buckle, but it had become loose and my hair brush, socks and tooth-paste spilled on to the path.

'Oh, Darren, if only you wouldn't try to be helpful,' Jane sighed as she returned with the head-collar. 'Look out. Stand clear.'

As Darren bent to retrieve my tooth mug Magic's sense of humour surfaced. I'd left my pony's reins free while I unloaded her and now I had my head under the saddle flap unfastening her girth. So I was taken by surprise when she stepped forward to nudge Darren gently, tipping him into a clump of hollyhocks outside the garden fence.

At the same time I lost my balance and sprawled on the cobbles.

'See what I mean.' Jane tried not to laugh. 'Whenever Darren helps, disaster is sure to follow!'

Sliding the head collar up her arm she bent to set her small brother on his feet.

'Be a good boy, Darren,' she told him, 'and stand over there. You can open the gate for Magic when we're ready to put her in the field. But don't touch it until I tell you. Understand?'

Darren couldn't manage to open the gate. The piece of wood that Jane used to wedge in the hasp fitted too tightly for his small fingers and his sister had to lend a hand.

'Thank goodness you've got a pony-proof catch,' I said. 'After what happened last night I don't want Magic to do any more escaping. Honestly, Jane, you wouldn't have thought any pony could do so much damage in ten minutes flat. And Mrs Farley was so nice about it. Oddly enough the only time she seemed really exasperated was when the police sergeant turned up in a squad car.'

'Squad car!' Jane echoed.

'Yes. Apparently one of the neighbours heard us shouting "Police" and telephoned the station.'

'Go on.' Jane was intrigued. 'Tell all.'

'Well, the sergeant made tea for everybody. Then he said today would be his day off and that he'd come round after breakfast and put in a morning tidying and re-sowing the vegetable patch and then replace the broken glass.'

'And what did Mrs Farley say about that?' Jane asked.

'That's what is so mystifying,' I told her. 'She just cut him short and said, "No thank you, Sergeant Hickson. I don't want to be under any obligation to you."'

'Poor Sergeant Hickson,' said Jane. 'He's so kind but Mrs Farley just flees from him.'

'But why?' I asked. 'Sergeant Hickson seems such a super sort of man.'

'Oh, he is, and maybe he and Mrs Farley will get married one day,' Jane explained, 'but not just yet. Mrs Farley's still knocked off balance by her husband's death.'

'Perhaps Sergeant Hickson shouldn't try to hurry her,' I speculated.

'That's what I thought,' Jane agreed. 'Then I

decided that Sergeant Hickson must be in a bit of a dilemma. He naturally wants to rally round and be protective towards Mrs Farley, especially after the burglary. He just can't keep away when she so obviously needs help.'

'On the other hand, if he does help, he can't hide his feelings,' I suggested, 'and that makes Mrs Farley imagine she's being rushed.'

'I suppose that's it,' Jane sighed. 'Oh, I do want things to go right for Mrs Farley. She's so pretty and kind and brave, and she certainly made her husband very happy. Sergeant Hickson was Bill Farley's best friend; and the sergeant himself has been very lonely these last two years since his wife was killed by a motor-bike.'

I nodded. 'I think he and Mrs Farley could be so happy together and, of course, it would solve the burglar problem. Villains would think twice about breaking into a shop with a police sergeant on the premises.'

'Well, let's hope for wedding bells in the spring.' Jane gave a short laugh. 'If you were still at the shop, Pippa, you could have helped things along by playing Cupid.'

'I wouldn't know how,' I said.

While Jane and I were talking we had been sitting on the bench outside the farmhouse, sipping lemonade in the sun. Now a pony squeal from the other side of the hedge brought us back to the sobering realisation that we were in sole charge of the Pony Farm.

Jane jumped to her feet at the interruption. 'Oh dear,' she sighed, gazing towards the field. 'What now? I sometimes feel I can't relax for a moment. Not only are the ponies Auntie Sue's main interest in life but most of her money is tied up in them.'

'I suppose so,' I panted as we hurried to the field. 'Pure-bred Exmoors must be valuable. They're a dying breed.'

'That's right,' Jane acknowledged over her shoulder. 'Auntie Sue's been buying mares for the past two years and now she's hoping to raise pure-blooded foals to sell to breeders abroad.'

From the field came more noise of pony panic. Amidst it was the sound I knew only too well — Magic's plaintive whinny!

'Oh, dear.' I tugged at the gate. 'Perhaps we oughtn't to have put my pony in with the others, after all.'

'It's on account of the foal,' Jane explained. 'Your Magic seems to have taken a fancy to him and his mother's making a fuss.'

Magic and the foal were half-hidden by bracken in the far corner of the field. The foal was nosing Magic's flanks and she was rasping him affectionately with her tongue. The other ponies stood a little way off, fascinated; but Bracken, the foal's mother, watched jealously, thrusting out her muzzle warningly and spying her chance to reclaim her offspring.

As Bracken ventured nearer, Magic stamped a hoof. Then Bracken charged forward, nipped

Magic on the shoulder and tried to drive the foal away from her. Taken by surprise, Magic lashed out with her heels at Bracken. Unfortunately she caught the foal on the hock.

With a squeal the leggy creature hobbled away.

'Oh! I'm afraid Magic's lamed him,' I said in distress. 'How terrible!'

Jane moved cautiously towards the foal to inspect the injury. 'Don't look so tragic, Pippa. It could be worse. At least she hasn't cracked a bone. I suppose the bump will come up like an egg but it will go down with rest.'

'Meanwhile shall I put Magic in another field?' I suggested, feeling guilty.

'I hope that won't be necessary,' said Jane. 'She'll probably get on well enough with the other mares if we move Bracken and Dandy. I'll put them in Little Paddock. Then Dandy will be forced to rest because there won't be so much room for him to try to canter around.'

She managed to give me an enouraging smile and suddenly I felt relieved. It was kind of Jane not to make a dramatic production over the accident. I was very lucky to have her as a friend and to be able to help with the Exmoors.

I hoped, though, that Magic wasn't going to turn out to be a problem at the Pony Farm as she had been at Mrs Farley's. At home my pony had given no trouble; she'd been calm and willing.

As though reading my thoughts Jane suddenly said: 'Magic's a really beautiful pony. You are

27

lucky to have her.'

'Yes,' I nodded, 'and she's usually so very well behaved. At home I've been trying to train her to do elementary dressage and she's really coming on quite well.'

I felt a glow of renewed confidence. Jane was prepared to think well of Magic. I hoped events would justify her faith.

The scent of the meadowsweet drifted from the hedgerow in Little Paddock. Then I noticed that Dandy's limp seemed to be easier as he followed his mother into his new surroundings. Bracken dropped her head to sample the grass and the foal's small ears pricked as he gazed about him. Everything was suddenly wonderful again. I had no premonition that it might not stay that way – not even when a horse-box rumbled up the lane towards us. A good-looking young man was at the wheel and Darren was sitting on the knee of a blonde young woman beside him.

'Who are these people?' Jane looked puzzled. 'I've never seen them before, and what's Darren doing with them?'

The horse-box pulled up and the young woman climbed down. Now that I could see her clearly I realised that there was something familiar about her face.

'I'm Micky's sister, Ruby,' the young woman announced chummily.

So that's why she looked familiar! I noted her tight jeans; the pony's head on her tee-shirt and a bracelet of horseshoe charms dangling from her wrist.

Chipped nail varnish was visible as she gestured towards the young man at her side.

'This is my boyfriend, Kevin.'

We gazed at the handsome, tall young man. Tight, dark curls crowded from under a leather cap. From beneath unusually long lashes, tawny hazel eyes regarded us challengingly, as though their owner through that we might resent his arrival.

We were both silent for a moment and then said in chorus: 'How do you do?' before breaking off into giggles and feeling a bit foolish.

'Hi!' Thumbs in the pockets of his tight Levi cords, Kevin looked down at us appraisingly. 'Two real pony girls if ever I've seen any. Nice to meet you both.' He gave us a flashing smile and then nodded towards the stable-cottage with its white-washed walls and window-boxes from which nasturtiums tumbled in a riot of orange and gold. 'So that's our pad, is it, Ruby?' He turned to the young woman at his side. 'Come on. Let's move in right away.'

'Now look here . . .' Jane began to protest but Ruby, with a rather artificial smile, forestalled her.

'We're not really gate-crashers. This'll explain why we're here.' She handed Jane an envelope. 'It's a note from Micky. He feels so bad about leaving you in the lurch that he wants to make amends. Go on, flower, read it. Then you'll understand.'

Dear Jane and Pippa,

I couldn't sleep a wink thinking how I'd let you down. So I got in touch with my sister, Ruby. She's a natural with ponies. It runs in the family, Dad and Grandad having been jockeys. Ruby's like me, always ready to do a good turn. So she's agreed to fill the gap and, if your Auntie Sue likes her, she could stay on. I forgot to give you the key of the cottage so I've handed it to Ruby. She'll do the cooking for you until our Mum can take over again. She makes a smashing steak pie.

I'm going to like it here. The other stable lads are a grand lot and I'll be looking after three horses — Arab Sheik's a chestnut and he's already won some races. Then there's a bay filly, Dream Morning — she's a bit flighty — and Green Jacket, who's getting on a bit now but still comes up in the money.
Still your pal, I hope,
Micky.
P.S. Here are two peace-offerings — one for you and one for Pippa.

Jane tipped up the envelope and two lucky horseshoe brooches fell into her palm.

'How kind of Micky,' I said.

Then Ruby broke into our thoughts with a bright smile.

'So here we are, petal,' she breezed, linking arms with Kevin. 'With all our worldly goods in a couple of suitcases and — don't faint, Jane — we've got three ponies in the horse-box!'

4

Too many ponies

'Three ponies!' I gasped. 'But where are we going to put them?'

'That's exactly what I was going to say,' Jane echoed.

'Worry not. We'll sort that out when I've got them unboxed,' breezed Ruby as she helped Kevin to let down the ramp.

We watched, intrigued, while Kevin scrambled inside and backed out a dapple grey.

'Meet Cobweb.' He handed the mare's halter to me. 'Make friends with her, while I get the other two.'

'Steady on,' I protested as Cobweb, scenting grass, nearly pulled me off my feet in an attempt to get to the field. 'We may have problems here. Ponies don't always take to each other, you know. My pony, Magic, has already caused trouble.'

'What's the hassle?' Ruby asked. 'You've got three fields.'

'Yes,' said Jane, 'but the Exmoors and Magic are in one. We've had to put Bracken and her foal in Little Paddock and the far field's fallow. It's got to be rested and treated so that the ponies don't get red worm.'

'Decisions! Decisions!' Kevin said lightly. 'Leave it to Rube and me. We'll sort it all out.'

'That's all very well,' Jane pointed out, 'but Auntie Sue's ponies are special. Pure-bred Exmoors are extremely rare. If it wasn't for Auntie Sue and one or two other breeders the strain might die out. That's why I don't think we ought to introduce other ponies into the field – not without a vet's certificate anyway.'

I swallowed, hoping that Magic wasn't sickening for anything catching. It was bad enough that she had accidentally kicked Bracken's foal.

'Of all the ungrateful girls!' Kevin's handsome face suddenly clouded in a flash of temper. 'Just making difficulties! Come on, Rube – put Cobweb back in the box and we'll be off. We're wasted here.'

'Oh, please, Kev. Don't be so hasty,' Ruby pleaded. 'These kids need help. And, anyway, it isn't right for them to be here on their own. We ought to stay.'

'You stay.' Kevin turned his back on Ruby who looked really distressed. 'I'm going.'

I was surprised to notice that Ruby was nearly in tears. She must be infatuated with Kevin, I thought, and suddenly I felt sorry for her.

Jane must have felt the same.

'I suppose we could take a chance on the ponies

being all right,' she said uneasily.

Ruby hugged her in quick relief. 'You won't regret it, petal — and don't think badly of Kevin. He's okay. Just goes off like a bottle of pop now and then, isn't that right, Kev?'

Kevin scrambled into the horse-box and backed out another mare. This one was plump but tired-looking. Her mid-brown coat was flecked with grey and so was her mealy muzzle and she had the light 'eye-spectacles' of the typical Exmoor.

'Queenie's as good as any of your Auntie's Exmoors,' Kevin assured Jane. 'I dare say your Auntie wouldn't mind buying this one for her stud. Tell you what . . . we'll let her have Queenie cheap in return for our accommodation, eh, Ruby?'

'The mare seems rather old,' Jane said. Then, feeling sorry for the weary-looking pony, she added, 'but I dare say she's sound enough.'

'That's right. Don't look a gift horse in the mouth, ducky,' Ruby said quickly.

Before Kevin could bring out the third pony, Ruby glanced towards Little Paddock where Dandy was limping after his mother.

'There's something wrong with that foal.' She walked to the gate. 'Let's see.'

We watched as Ruby quietly approached the mother. She held out her fingers for the foal to sniff before running her hands gently over the injured hock. There was no doubt about it: Ruby had a way with ponies.

'Hmm,' she said after a moment. 'This is coming

up into a nasty lump. The foal's got a bad bruise.'
She turned to Jane. 'If he was older I'd suggest
cold fomentations. As it is, we might try trickling a
hose over his hock.'

'What about Bracken?' Jane looked doubtful.
'She might think her foal was threatened.'

'She won't. Will you, old girl?' Ruby rubbed the
mare between the eyes. 'You've got enough sense
to know when somebody's trying to help you.' She
turned again to Jane. 'Put a halter on the mother
and bring her to the stable-yard. She'll be less fussy
if she can see what we're doing.'

Sure enough, Ruby's judgment proved sound.
Bracken stood quietly with Jane, watching while
Ruby held the foal and I trickled cold water
steadily over his hock.

Kevin, meanwhile, leaned against the horse-
box, surprisingly sucking a toffee apple. Darren
was doing the same. Apparently the two were
getting on well.

Suddenly, from inside the horse-box, there came
the stamping of a pony hoof, followed by an
imperious neigh.

'Firebird!' Ruby looked up from the foal. 'He
wonders why he's been left in the box. Bring him
out, Kev.' She turned to us. 'He's a stallion.'

'A stallion!' echoed Jane. 'Now she tells me!' She
raised her eyes to heaven. 'We can't have a stallion
here with Auntie Sue's pure-bred Exmoor mares.'

'That's right, petal. Firebird will have to go in
the stable.'

She called to her boyfriend: 'Carry on, Kev.'

To our surprise, instead of the spirited animal we had expected, Firebird turned out to be almost as elderly as Queenie.

Sunken-backed and rheumy-eyed, his appearance certainly gave the lie to his name. Yet, once unboxed, he caught sight of the mares across the yard and, arching his rheumaticky old neck, called to them shrilly.

'Come on, you old warrior!' Kevin tugged at Firebird's halter rope and, with a slap on the rump, led him towards the loose-box.

'Pippa! Jane!' Ruby turned briskly to us. 'Rustle up some straw and a water-bucket so that we can get his lordship bedded down.'

'I didn't think he'd be so old,' I said, tactless in my disappointment.

'He may be getting on a bit.' Ruby was quick to defend Firebird. 'But he's not over the hill. He'll sire many a good foal yet. I've got a soft spot for the old rascal. But then I'm daft about all horses. That's how I came to be lumbered with three. Kev gave me Firebird just last week – a birthday present! I've had Cobweb since she was a two-year-old. As for Queenie – well, she might have gone for dog-meat if I hadn't offered her a home.'

She looked across at the plump Exmoor who was now grazing with Magic and the other mares.

'What I don't understand,' I puzzled, 'is why a typical Exmoor like Queenie should be in danger of going for meat. If there's a scarcity of the breed,

I'd have thought that she'd be more valuable alive than dead.'

'True enough,' Ruby acknowledged. 'But you see, petal, Queenie really is old – pushing twenty-five or so. Definitely too old to have any more foals.'

Later, while Jane and I were getting lunch ready, we could see, through the kitchen window, Kevin carrying two suitcases across the yard towards the stable-cottage while Ruby followed, her arms full of clothes.

'I like Ruby better than Kevin,' Jane said doubtfully, patting the lettuce dry with some kitchen paper. 'He's too good-looking to be trusted.'

At that moment Ruby looked in our direction. 'Any nosh going spare?' she called hopefully. 'Kev and I are starving.'

'You'd better lay five places, Pippa,' Jane said resignedly.

* * * *

'This is really kind of you, petal.' Ruby patted Jane's shoulder as she sat down at the kitchen table.

'All very matey.' Kevin was now relaxed as he helped himself to ham, lettuce and tomato. 'You're out to help us and we're out to help you.' He glanced towards the window. 'It's gone dark. Switch the light on, somebody. I can't see whether

I'm eating caterpillars or lettuce.'

The light bulb flickered and there was a sudden flash outside, followed by a roll of thunder.

'The storm's almost overhead.' Ruby spoke above the rattle of raindrops on the window pane. 'We got our gear under cover just in time.'

'But we opened the bedroom window in the cottage,' Kevin exclaimed, peering through the steamy rivulets. He jerked his head at Ruby. 'The bed will be soaked. You'd better go and see to it, Rube.'

'Oh, men!' Ruby grabbed a mac from a peg on the back door and plunged through the downpour. 'Talk about useless!'

She was back a few moments later, dripping wetly over the tiled floor.

'There's something wrong with one of the ponies.' She looked seriously at us. 'I could see from the yard.'

'Which one?' I asked quickly, my heart missing a beat.

'Well, it's not one of the Exmoors . . .'

'Go on,' I urged.

'It's the chestnut mare that looks as though she's got a bit of Arab blood.'

Magic? Oh, no!

'She's huddled with the others under the trees,' said Ruby, 'and she's kicking at her stomach. You know what that means?'

'Yes,' I said with dread, rushing to the window. 'Magic's got colic!'

5

Magic's ordeal

Through the rain-streaked window pane, I gazed at my pony in dismay.

In the field across the yard Magic was looking sorry for herself. She was standing awkwardly, head down, and lifting a hind foot to kick in an irritable way at her swollen intestine.

'It must be all that soft fruit she ate when she broke into Mrs Farley's garden last night,' I groaned.

Jane nodded numbly. 'She certainly looks poorly.'

'I'll call the vet,' I decided.

'Yes,' Jane nodded, 'but first let's move her under cover.'

'That's right, ducks.' Ruby rubbed her sleeve over the misty glass to gaze at the farm-buildings. 'But Firebird's in your only loose-box. Is there anywhere else with enough room for us to keep her on the move so that she won't try to roll and twist her gut?'

'In the barn.' Jane grabbed her mac from a peg and handed me a heavy yellow oilskin. 'This is

Auntie Sue's but she won't mind, I hope. Put it on and come quickly. There's no time to waste. Ruby, you phone the vet. He'll take more notice of a grown-up.'

I struggled into the oilskin and plunged after Jane into the heavy rain. In the field Magic was moving her feet restlessly. She looked as if, at any moment, she might go down and roll.

I broke into a run. 'Come on, Magic.' I caught my pony's head-collar to lead her towards the barn. 'We'll soon have you warm and dry.'

In the barn Jane took my pony's head while I grabbed a handful of straw to wisp her down. Magic's breathing seemed jerky. Already she had broken into a sweat and her eyes seemed tinged with red.

'Oh dear, she's really ill.' I broke off my wisping to turn to Jane. 'I wonder if there's anything else we can do before the vet comes.'

'I don't know.' Jane looked distressed. 'If only Auntie Sue were here! Or even Micky. I just haven't had enough pony experience to help.'

Magic looked round and again started to hoof irritably at her gut. Then she tried to lie down and it took both Jane and me all our strength to get her to take a step forward.

Meanwhile I racked my brain to remember all I had read about colic. 'Sometimes,' I said, 'people tie a hot rolled-up blanket under the pony to ease the pain.'

'Just as we'd use a hot water bottle for tummy-ache,' added Jane.

I nodded. 'Oh, if only I'd got my *First-Aid Hints for Pony-Owners*.'

Jane looked up as we heard running footsteps in the yard. 'Here comes Ruby. She might have some good ideas to tide us over until the vet comes.'

'Sorry, petals.' Ruby's face was flushed and her hair hung in lank streaks. 'I couldn't get through to the vet. The line is dead. It must be the storm. But Kev and I can drive down to the surgery in the horse-box and tell the vet to come right away. How's that, flower?'

'Oh, Ruby, you are a godsend,' I thanked her.

Magic shifted her feet. This time we were not quick enough to stop her lying down.

'Get her up!' Ruby hurried to lend a hand. 'Don't let her roll. Come on, beauty. Ups-a-daisy! There's a girl!'

My pony let herself be coaxed back to her feet and we all breathed freely again.

'Better spread some straw around so that she doesn't scrape her knees.' Ruby turned from Jane to me. 'Ponies with colic often lie down and get up again but, whatever happens, you mustn't let Magic roll.'

She broke off as a toot came from the horse-box in the yard.

'Coming, Kev.' She turned to us. 'Got to go now, ducks.'

Magic shifted her shoulders as though she was going to lie down yet again but Jane tugged at her head and managed to stop her.

'Get on the other side, Pippa,' she said breath-lessly. 'Let's try walking her up and down. That might help to ease the wind. As long as she's walking she can't lie down.'

It seemed an age before Jane and I persuaded Magic to parade round the barn. My pony kept trying to pull her head away. I suppose she wanted to look round to see what was the matter with her swollen flanks.

'Poor Magic,' I soothed. 'Sorry, girl, but you must keep going. It's for your own good.'

About half-an-hour later the barn door burst open. A bedraggled Darren scampered inside. He was wearing his sou'wester but his mac only half-covered his shoulders and his feet were wet in their sandals.

'Telephone!' he piped. 'The bell's ringing in a funny way.'

'I'll go.' Jane ran to the door, calling back over her shoulder as she sped towards the house. 'Stay with Pippa, Darren.'

'What's wrong with Magic?' Darren asked me.

'A very serious kind of tummy ache,' I explained. 'She's eaten too much fruit.'

Darren nodded his sou'westered head. 'I got tummy ache last summer when I ate too many green apples. Poor Magic.' He reached up a grubby hand to pat my pony's shoulder. Magic flinched.

'Don't touch her, Darren,' I warned him. 'She

41

just wants to be left alone.'

A few minutes later Jane appeared, looking really troubled. 'More bad news, Pippa. Ruby was on the phone. She said the horse-box has broken down and they haven't been able to get to Mr Corrin, the vet, after all. I tried to ring him but there's something wrong with the phone. Although Ruby was able to ring us, the line sounded very faint and by the time I tried the vet's number the line had gone dead. I suppose people can ring us, but we can't make any out-going calls. It happens sometimes.'

'What are we going to do?' Magic's breathing was now very raspy and I felt really desperate. 'There's only one thing for it,' I decided. 'If we can't get the vet to visit Magic, she'll have to go to him.'

'Through all this?' Jane glanced at the open door where rain, which had now flooded part of the stable yard, was splashing off the cobbles into the straw of the barn.

'It's the only way,' I decided. 'At least Magic will be kept moving. We can take it slowly. It might even do her some good. I once read about a girl whose pony had colic and she saved its life by walking it around all night.'

Jane looked doubtful. 'That might work when a pony has only a mild colic, I suppose. But Magic does look dreadful and the rain's torrential. I really think she shouldn't get wet.'

'Have you got a New Zealand rug?' I asked.

Jane shook her head. 'The Exmoors are so hardy they don't need anything like that.' Desperately she looked round the barn. 'Auntie Sue's oilskin cape!' she exclaimed. 'We could put it over Magic's back, unbuckle the reins from one of the spare bridles and use it as a surcingle.'

'Good thinking!' I said. Then I felt dismay again. 'Wouldn't the fastening be too tight under Magic's tummy?'

'Well, you needn't pull the strap too tight,' Jane pointed out. 'We could thread another piece of leather through the button-hole at the neck of the cape. That would help to keep everything in place. Besides, at the pace that you'll be going, it might not slip round.'

'It's worth a try,' I nodded.

Suddenly we heard the sound of a match being struck and Jane swooped down on her young brother. 'Darren! What do you think you're doing? Where did you get those matches?'

'I brought them from the kitchen.' Darren became tearful at Jane's tone as she blew out the flame. He fished in the pocket of his mac and brought out a stumpy candle. 'The candles were in the cupboard under the sink. I knew Auntie Sue kept them there. It's gone so dark that I thought you might like a light in the barn.'

'Never do anything like that again.' Jane took the matches and candle from him. 'You must never play with matches, Darren.' She gave him a shake. '*Never!*'

She looked desperately from her small brother to me. 'You see how it is, Pippa. I don't like letting you walk through the storm by yourself with Magic being so ill, but I couldn't possibly leave Darren here on his own. He might set the place on fire! Goodness knows what he might think of next.'

Jane glanced helplessly at me as I led my sick pony to the doorway.

'Oh, Pippa.' She sounded really worried. 'It's dreadful for you to have to go alone. Do you think you can manage?'

I sighed heavily. 'I've no choice. So wish me luck, Jane. I'm sure I'm going to need it!'

6

For love of a pony

When we reached the barn door, Magic jibbed at the rain so I had to tug her into the yard while Jane pushed her quarters.

'You *must* try to walk,' I urged my pony. 'Your life may depend on it.'

Rivulets ran down my neck and up my sleeves as I led my sick and unwilling pony down the lane. At the main road a car slushed past, spattering us with muddy water and making Magic flinch. After that, my pony just didn't seem to care what happened to her.

She moved forward mechanically, head hung dismally. Occasionally her sides heaved and she grunted with pain.

I think that if I had let go of her head she would have lain down on the road.

'Oh, please, Magic,' I begged. 'Don't give up!'

After a while her breathing seemed easier. She was walking less stiffly and – wretched though the journey was in the rain-soaked gloom – I began to feel that keeping her moving really was helping.

'There's a beauty.' I straightened Magic's wet

mane and stroked her neck encouragingly. 'Keep on trying. We're halfway there.'

My hopes ebbed again as the rain pelted harder. I began to feel as miserable as my pony looked. How had we got ourselves into this trouble, I asked myself desperately.

If only Mummy and Daddy were here to help. Perhaps I ought to have phoned them to let them know that I was taking Magic and staying at the Pony Farm instead of remaining with Mrs Farley in Abbot's Coombe as they'd expected. Probably they'd have tried to stop me which, I suppose, was why I didn't ring them.

But they'd have been right! I realised that now. It would have been easier to cope with a sick pony in the field behind the village shop. Mrs Farley could have helped and the vet would have been nearby. Well, it was no good thinking like that. Here we were and we'd just got to make the best of it.

Meanwhile the road had dropped to lower ground. Mud and water from the sodden fields oozed across the tarmac, leaving a skiddy surface. I could hardly keep on my feet and Magic's hooves were sliding dangerously. The river lay ahead and now I could hear the roar of an angry torrent. We rounded a bend and I saw that the water in the ford had spread to almost the width of a lake. The splintered rails of the footbridge showed above the eddies but the planks were hidden.

Defeated and in tears I realised that we could

not possibly get across. What could we do now? There was no other route to Abbot's Coombe and the vet.

'Sorry, Magic.' I leant my head against my pony's sodden neck. 'I've brought you all this way only to make things worse for you. Now we'll have to go back.'

I had barely turned my pony when I heard the rumble of falling rocks and a stone wall beside the road came crashing down ahead of us. Stones, earth and flowing mud cascaded across to make a barrier between ourselves and our return route.

We were trapped!

I glanced round desperately. In Magic's weak state I didn't think she could possibly negotiate the stones and rubble; nor could I attempt to swim her across the deeply-flooded ford.

I felt near to tears again. 'I've let you down, Magic,' I groaned. 'I've been foolhardy and silly. It's all my fault.'

Just then my pony's ears quivered and she turned her head. She had been the first to hear the rumble of an approaching vehicle – a cattle truck.

It skidded to a stop a few inches from the rocks. A young man and a boy jumped from the cab. Their freckled features and red hair made me realise that they were probably brothers. Sympathetically they stared from the landslide to Magic and me.

'In trouble?' asked one.

I nodded, trying not to look helpless. 'My pony's sick and I was trying to take her to the vet but the footbridge is under water and we can't get across the ford. We're stranded.'

Working with desperate speed, the two boys used tyre levers to roll away the worst of the boulders. They cleared a path so that – almost by a miracle –the elder boy managed to edge the cattle truck bumpily to where Magic and I were standing.

The boys let down the ramp and now I was able to help as we coaxed, tugged and shoved Magic aboard.

The younger boy and I stayed in the back of the truck with Magic, trying to hold her steady, while the elder boy drove slowly over the stones and then – with a *whoosh* – navigated the ford. Soon we were clear of the water, on higher ground.

'I'll never be able to thank you two enough,' I told Jimmy as we supported Magic between us. 'You're wonderful. You both seemed to know exactly the right thing to do.'

'Our Dad's taught us how to deal with emergencies.' Jimmy gave a modest smile. 'He's an expert. He's in the police force.'

I raised my brows in amazement as I realised there was something familiar about the boys' features and their vivid hair, now darkened to red-setter colour by the rain. 'By some strange coincidence, does your father happen to be Sergeant Hickson?'

Jimmy nodded, a friendly smile on his freckled face as he gestured towards his brother in the cab.

'That's right – Jimmy and George Hickson – at your service.' He peered through the slats of the truck. 'Won't be long now. The vet's place is just over the hill.'

* * * *

The Hickson brothers stood by as the vet gave Magic a thorough examination.

'She needs an injection and a long rest some-where warm and dry,' the vet decided. 'We'll have to keep her here.'

I nodded, relieved.

'That's settled then.' The vet looked across to George and Jimmy. 'Can you two give me a hand to bed the pony down in one of my loose-boxes? I'll tie her up so that she can't roll,' he explained to me, 'but really I think the worst of the colic is over. It's chill that we must guard against now.'

George and Jimmy hurried ahead, under the vet's direction, to put down the straw. Then the vet and I led Magic to her temporary abode. Once inside, I gently wisped down my pony and said goodnight.

'Be good, Magic. I'm not forsaking you. I'll be back in the morning to see how you are. All you have to do is to rest and get better.'

'That's right.' The vet shut the loose-box door. He turned to George Hickson. 'By the way, George, I haven't seen you driving a cattle truck before. Have you started work on one of the farms round here?'

'No,' said George. 'I'm working with Jackson Swift, the dealer. This is the firm's truck. As a matter of fact, Jimmy and I have been to Moorcroft to pick up some sheep for the trials.'

'Where are they then?' puzzled the vet. 'You can't have dropped them off before you got to the river.'

'They weren't at Moorcroft either.' Jimmy's eyes widened as he told us. 'They were missing. The farmer had brought them down ready for trucking and they'd vanished into thin air. Stolen!'

'Yes,' George confirmed. 'The farmer said they were there in his home field this afternoon. Then, about five o'clock when the storm got torrential, he put them into an empty barn behind the farmyard. The road passes the barn and he thought it would be easier for loading, with there being such a downpour. Anyway, some time between five and half past six when we arrived to pick them up, some villains had lifted them.'

'They must have driven up in another truck,' said Jimmy. 'Perhaps they'd been watching the farm all day. Then, seeing the farmer putting the sheep in the barn, they realised it was their best chance to steal them. The barn's out of sight of the house. So, with the farmer and his wife having their tea in the kitchen and it thundering and lightning as it was just then, the villains could have taken the whole flock of sheep and nobody was the wiser.'

'Does your Dad know about this?' enquired the vet.

George shook his head. 'We were on our way to tell him when we met this young lady in distress.'

'Well, we'd better alert your father right away.' The vet led the way to the house. 'The phone lines may be mended now.'

They weren't.

So the Hickson boys still weren't able to tell the police about the missing sheep.

'We'll have to drive to the police station,' announced George. Then he turned to me. 'But what do we do about you?'

I looked blank. 'How do you mean?'

'Well, we can't risk driving you home across the ford. The water's deepening all the time and we might all get stuck.'

'Could you drop me off at Mrs Farley's shop then?' I asked.

'Will do,' George said cheerfully.

'Hop in.' Jimmy helped me into the cab. Then he pulled at the lobe of his right ear as he sat beside me. 'My ear's itching. That always means we're in for a few surprises. It never fails!'

7

S.O.S. from Jane

I never expected Jimmy's first surprise to happen so quickly!

Fifteen minutes after he had told me about his itching ear I was astonished to see Sergeant Hickson, jacket off, sandbagging a door to prevent the rising flood from swirling into the Corner Sh

George pulled up and jumped from the cab.

'I was on my way to the police station to see you, Dad. Sorry to take you off this good deed, but there's been some villainy you ought to know about.'

He reported the missing sheep.

'You see, Dad,' Jimmy added 'they must have been stolen.'

'Right!' Sergeant Hickson dropped the half-filled sandbag and walked to his car, saying over his shoulder: 'We'll put out a call over the R.T. to alert the patrols. Tell Mrs Farley I'll be back as soon as possible to finish off the sandbagging.'

'No, please, Tom. You've enough to do.' Mrs Farley, overhearing, came to the door. 'Dave and Pete will fill the rest of the sandbags after they've helped me move the perishable stock.'

'I'll be along just the same, Tessa,' said Sergeant Hickson, undaunted.

Mrs Farley sighed. 'Oh, dear, I thought you might say that, Tom. It's very kind of you but it will only start tongues wagging if you keep coming round here.'

The sergeant smiled. 'Sorry, Tessa, but I can't leave you to tackle this lot.'

'We'll manage,' Mrs Farley said, and added in a bantering tone, 'Now, be off with you, Tom Hickson. Get after those missing sheep. That's what we pay our rates for.'

As the sergeant drove off, Jimmy Hickson gave Mrs Farley a cheeky grin.

'Give Dad a break, Mrs Farley,' he said lightly. 'Life would be wonderful if only you two would get married.'

George entered into the spirit of the banter. 'Yes, and then we could have your apple pie every Sunday.'

'And we could call you Mum!' Jimmy added with a twinkle.

'You two are as bad as your father!' Mrs Farley's cheeks were quite pink with embarrassment. 'Be off with you!'

*   *   *   *

'Woof! Woof!'

I woke to hear Glen's bark. What was

happening? Where was I? Then I remembered that I was in the big bedroom above the Corner Shop. The rising flood had prevented me getting back to the Pony Farm.

'Are you awake, Pippa?' came Mrs Farley's voice from the other bed. I was sharing with her because Pete and Dave, having been rained out of their tent, were now in the spare room.

'Don't panic! It's not burglars,' came my brother's voice from the landing. 'The telephone's been tinkling. Dave's gone down to see if anyone's trying to get through.'

'There's no one at the other end,' Dave reported up the stairs. 'I suppose the engineers are trying to repair the line.'

'Go back to bed then,' said Mrs Farley.

Throughout the night the telephone tinkled from time to time and Glen gave answering woofs from the scullery.

It wasn't until dawn that I fell completely asleep and then only for a short time, it seemed, because the telephone suddenly rang loudly and continually.

So the lines had been repaired.

I was the first downstairs. As I picked up the receiver Jane's voice came faintly over the crackling wires.

'Is that you, Pippa? I've been trying to telephone you all night . . . What's been happening?'

'Magic's okay,' I told her quickly. 'She's bedded

down at the vet's.'

Jane sounded breathless. 'I was worried about you, Pippa. But that's not the only reason I'm phoning. I'm in trouble here. Ruby and Kevin haven't come back. Darren's got a cough and I don't like to leave him alone in the house – and the ponies . . .'

She was suddenly cut off in mid-sentence.

'What's happened to the ponies? Jane! Are you there, Jane?' I jiggled the telephone rest but the line stayed dead. There wasn't even the usual dialling tone.

Frantically I looked up the Pony Farm number. I dialled it but without result.

'Oh dear!' I turned to Pete who was now by my side. 'The engineers must have managed to mend the wires but now there's another fault. And it sounds as if something's terribly wrong at the Pony Farm. I've got to get back there!'

'Not without your breakfast,' said Mrs Farley.

'Can't stop for food.' I bounded upstairs to scramble into my clothes. 'Sorry, Mrs Farley. Can I borrow your bike?'

I pulled on my jeans and sweater, wheeled Mrs Farley's bicycle from the back kitchen and lifted it over the sandbags into the muddy road.

'Hey, Pippa!' came a muffled shout from my brother who, halfway down the stairs, was tugging his polo-neck sweater over his head. 'Wait for Dave and me.'

As I turned to say: 'Can't stop', the kitchen door

burst open and an excited flurry of black-and-white nosed its way through. In my haste I hadn't latched the door and now Glen was at large and raring to go.

'Come back, Glen,' I shouted as the sheepdog bounded over the sandbags to investigate the morning smells.

'Glen!' shouted Pete while, from the landing, Dave gave a shrill whistle.

For once, though, Glen wasn't prepared to be an obedient, trial-trained sheepdog. He'd been penned up all night and now he was ready to run off his high spirits.

'Back, Glen,' I scolded, pointing to the open doorway. But Glen just jumped to lick my chin.

'You bad dog!' Pete caught him with a rugby tackle.

So, leaving my brother rolling with the dog in a mock-wrestle, I pedalled off down the road.

I had only just turned into the next street when Glen's excited bark sounded behind me again. The dog must have broken loose and, not to be done out of a run, was now racing alongside.

'You're a help, I don't think,' I scolded him. I wobbled and skidded to avoid the bounding dog. 'Go back to Dave.'

Glen didn't want to understand. He was enjoying his run and he was more than ready for a swim when we reached the ford. He thought it was a grand game when I rolled up my jeans and, half-carrying the bicycle, inched my way along the submerged planks of the footbridge.

The next quarter of a mile was downhill and I was able to free-wheel with Glen panting beside the bicycle. It was quarter-past seven by my watch when I rode through the gate of the Pony Farm.

'Thank goodness you're here, Pippa,' Jane gasped. 'Darren's so fretful that I thought I'd better keep him indoors, and goodness knows where the ponies have got to.'

We were about to go to the field to see where the animals had broken out when Jane suddenly stopped in her tracks and pointed across the grass.

'The stream!' she exclaimed, staring. 'Where's it gone? The water-course is dry.'

I followed her gaze, flabbergasted. In spite of all the flooding there was not a sign of water where the stream had been. Instead there was just a wide and muddy ditch.

It all seemed very mysterious. First the ponies and then the stream disappearing! Was this Jimmy's surprise Number Two?

'I simply don't understand it,' I puzzled. 'With all that rain there should be more water not less. It's uncanny!'

8

Where are the ponies?

'I just don't know where to start looking.' Jane gazed across the pony-less field in dismay.

'They've probably made a gap and broken out,' I said.

Before we could begin to search, a Range Rover turned into the yard and, to our astonishment, we saw Mrs Farley at the wheel. Previously I'd seen her only on a bicycle and I didn't realise she could drive.

As Glen ran barking to the Range Rover I saw that Mrs Farley wasn't alone. Dave and Pete were in the back.

'Hello, Mrs Farley,' Jane gasped as we ran towards her. 'Why aren't you at the shop?'

'I thought you might need help here so I put a notice on the door saying BACK AT ELEVEN. The boys and I have come to lend a hand. What's happened?'

'Oh, you are a brick, Mrs Farley,' Jane exclaimed. 'We didn't know where to start. It would be a terrific help if you'd stay with Darren and answer any telephone calls. The ponies are missing, so the rest of us could try to track them down.'

'Good idea!' nodded Dave. He gazed round the field. 'Now, before we start dashing round in all directions, let's think this out.'

Pete agreed. 'That's right. The bank might have broken somewhere upstream and diverted the water.'

'But what's that to do with the ponies?' I puzzled.

'Perhaps everything.' Pete pointed to the dried stream-bed. 'There's nothing left there but mud. The ponies would be parched for a drink. They could have broken out to find water.'

'Good thinking!' said Jane. 'Come on.'

With Glen bounding ahead, we set off at a run.

'The ponies went this way,' Dave said a few minutes later. 'You can see where they've broken down the hedge. There's a gap beside the stream-bed.'

Squeezing through, we followed the ponies' tracks along the muddy bank.

We crossed a lane beside a bridge and nose to the ground, Glen made for a gate across the lane. He wriggled through the bars and, as we climbed over to follow him, we saw the ponies' path trampled through a wheat field. Keeping to the edge, so as not to do any further damage, we panted after Glen.

On the far side of the field the land started to climb towards the moor. Beside a bracken-covered hill we caught the glint of water. Then, as we ran on, we heard the sound of a waterfall and saw the stream cascading down in a new course.

Dave pointed to four drunkenly-leaning wooden stakes and some strewn sheets of corrugated iron through which the water had broken. 'They've evidently had trouble here before. The farmer must have tried to repair the bank, but this time the force of the water has been too much for it.'

We stared at the stream as it left the hillside to pour into a drainage ditch in a small oak-wood below the hill.

'I suppose the stream will force its way through to join the river somewhere else,' speculated Jane.

Pete nodded. 'It looks as though the water's taking a short-cut. Maybe the stream ran this way long ago and then a farmer diverted it to water his land.'

Dave agreed. 'I'd say this is the natural course.' He climbed over the fence into the copse.

'That's all very well.' I stared all around. 'But where are the ponies? I can't see any down here.'

As if to answer my question Glen gave a woof and we saw that he was gazing up the hillside.

'Glen's spotted them!' Dave climbed back over the fence. 'The ponies didn't follow the stream through the wood. They probably had a drink above the waterfall and then moved on to the moor.'

Pete peered into the sunlight following Glen's gaze. Suddenly he pointed towards the shoulder of the hill. 'Is that a pony beside that thorn tree or is it a shadow?'

We shaded our eyes to search.

'Nothing there,' I said and then bit back my words as, quite distinctly, I saw the outline of a pony on the skyline. Screwing up my eyes, I gazed round to see three others. 'There they are!'

'If we rush they might scatter,' said Pete.

Dave nodded. 'Let's see what Glen can do. Here, boy,' he called the sheepdog to heel, then ordered him to sit.

Head on one side, ears pricked, Glen watched his master. What now?

Dave swept his arm towards the ponies. 'Go, Glen,' he ordered. 'Bring them in.'

The sheepdog streaked over the heather.

When Glen neared the leading pony Dave stopped him with a whistle; then he sent him in a wide arc to find and collect the others.

Soon Glen was hidden by the bracken. A whinny signalled that the ponies were approaching.

First one pony head, then another and a third appeared above the bracken. Steadily and surely Glen collected all the ponies and started to drive them down the hillside. Now they were all trotting towards us.

Suddenly Russet stopped. Apparently she saw us and decided she didn't want to be caught. With a toss of her head she shied away. Then, kicking up her heels, she broke into a canter and again made for the open moor.

Glen sped, ears flattened, body low, to outflank her. In front of the mare he dropped to the ground, staring hard at her as if to defy her to move.

Laying back her ears threateningly, Russet made for the dog. Glen still didn't move. He waited until the mare was almost upon him and then jumped up in front of her.

Russet's nerve snapped. She turned tail and cantered back to the others. Triumphantly Glen drove the little herd down the hill.

Pete grabbed Russet's forelock and held her as Glen, tongue lolling, returned to his master's side.

'Well done, Glen!' Dave made much of his dog.

We slipped the halters over the ponies' heads, scrambled onto them and rode bare-back to the Pony Farm. There were four of us and seven ponies, so Jane rode the wayward Russet and led Bumble and Queenie while I rode Ruby's Cobweb and led Heather.

Back at the Pony Farm we tied the ponies in the yard while we worked to repair the gap in the hedge. Dave and Pete found a drinking trough in the orchard and trundled it on a barrow to the field.

'We'll have to keep the trough filled from buckets for the time being,' said Dave. 'When Jane's Aunt gets back she'll be able to get a pipe laid.'

'I don't want to hurry you.' Mrs Farley came across the field with Darren. 'But it's ten past eleven.'

'And your notice said "Back at Eleven",' I remembered. 'Oh dear! I hope your customers won't be getting impatient and going to the supermarket.'

Dave tipped a final bucketful of water into the trough. 'We're ready now, Mrs Farley.'

'And thank you for your help,' Jane said gratefully as we all walked to the Range Rover.

'I wasn't able to do much after all.'

'You looked after Darren,' Jane pointed out. 'That's one person's full-time job.'

Dave and Pete piled into the Range Rover with Glen and Jane suddenly said: 'We'll come with you. We need to get some groceries.'

'Yes,' I added, 'and I'm longing to call at the vet's to see how Magic is.'

Before we left the yard there sounded the cheerful blast of a horn and a red Post Office van splashed through the puddles of the lane.

'Two for you, Jane.' The chatty postman tipped back his cap. 'This letter-card's from your Auntie by the look of the Rock of Gibraltar on the back. Some people have all the luck.'

He drove off and Jane read aloud to us: *By the time you get this, I shall be in Athens. I'm having a fantastic time, seeing all the places I've only read about. Imagine me having my photograph taken with the apes on the Rock! And before that there was Lisbon. Naples next, and the Isle of Capri. This really is the holiday of a lifetime. Your loving Aunt, Sue. P.S. I haven't a care in the world knowing the ponies are in such good hands.*

'Ignorance is bliss,' sighed Jane. 'Good old Auntie! If only she knew what calamities we've been having and that we're minus Micky!'

'And saddled with Kevin,' I added. There was something about Ruby's boyfriend that I just didn't like.

Meanwhile Jane was opening the other letter.

'It's from Micky!' Her eyes lit up as she scanned the scrawly note: *This is to let you know that I may be getting a day off soon. Don't know when. It depends on the stable roster. I'll pop over to see you. I'm having a great time. I ride Green Jacket at gallops. He's a bay gelding, nearly sixteen hands and he's quite a character – likes his polo mints. Love to you, Rube and Pippa from your old pal, Micky.*

'Nice of him to write,' I said.

Jane nodded. 'Perhaps his conscience is troubling him.'

By now we were at the ford and Mrs Farley slowed down to negotiate it. I suddenly found myself scratching my ear.

'Funny!' I exclaimed. 'My ear's itching. I wonder if I've caught it from Jimmy and if it means there's yet another surprise ahead.'

9

What a cheek!

'Odd!' Mrs Farley gazed in puzzlement at the door of her shop. 'My notice seems to have gone. I hung it on a hook as usual but, instead of it reading CLOSED, I sellotaped BACK AT ELEVEN on the card.'

'It must have blown down,' said Pete. 'Perhaps we forgot to shut the back door and that made a draught.'

'I know the back door was shut,' Dave said. He turned to Mrs Farley. 'I remember you locking and bolting it.'

'That's right.' Mrs Farley looked worried. 'I've been particularly careful about that ever since the break-in.'

She walked almost hesitantly to the shop door and turned the key. The door wouldn't budge.

'Perhaps it's swollen with the rain,' said Jane.

Mrs Farley shook her head. She looked defeated. 'No. It's burglars again, and they've bolted me out of my own shop!'

'In broad daylight?' I gasped. 'Surely not?'

'Thieves are cheeky enough for anything these

days.' Mrs Farley sounded bitter. 'Besides, the back of the shop isn't overlooked. The apple trees and raspberry canes screen it. Anybody could have broken a window and got in without being seen.'

Dave started towards the alley way. 'We'll soon see.'

With Dave gripping Glen's collar the boys led the way to the back of the shop. The back door was swinging wide open and nearby a shattered pane from the kitchen window showed how an entry had been gained.

We crowded inside to look at the chaos. The drawer of the till was open and empty. Spaces on the shelves showed where cartons of cigarettes and chocolates were missing. A jar of humbugs had been knocked over and the contents trodden into the linoleum. Three toffee apples were strewn across the counter.

'Oh dear!' Mrs Farley looked agonised. 'The mess is nearly as bad as last time and they've taken money from the till and pounds' worth of stock. Yet they say lightning never strikes twice in the same place! This really is terrible. How am I going to cope?'

'With the help of friends,' said Pete.

'You've gone quite pale,' added Jane. 'You're suffering from shock. Sit down, Mrs Farley, and I'll make you a cup of tea.'

'And I'll phone the police,' said Dave.

'Ask for Sergeant Hickson,' Mrs Farley told

him. 'Tell him that this time I really do need his help.'

* * * *

'Try not to worry too much, Mrs Farley,' Pete comforted when the sergeant and his constable had left later that morning. 'The orchard's still too wet for camping so Dave and I will be sleeping indoors to be near you.'

'That's very kind of you, Pete.' Bravely, Mrs Farley was trying not to give way to despair. 'But Sergeant Hickson particularly wanted his two boys to sleep here. You and Dave should be at the Pony Farm, helping Jane and Pippa.'

'That means we'll have to cycle in to the sheep-dog trials every morning,' said Dave.

'Oh, there won't be any trials for a day or two,' Mrs Farley assured him. 'The field will be under water.'

'So that settles that.' I moved to the doorway. 'Now perhaps we can go and visit Magic.' All morning I'd been longing to call at the vet's.

'Yes. You go and see Magic, Pippa.' Dave clipped on Glen's lead. 'Pete and I will inspect the trials ground.'

'Darren and I will stay here and help Mrs Farley get straight,' said Jane.

'That's right,' nodded Dave. 'Let's meet here at a quarter to one. Then we can all catch the bus back to the Pony Farm.'

* * * *

The vet was on his rounds when I reached the surgery but his wife was there, tidying up, sterilising instruments and keeping an eye on the three cats and one miniature Sealyham who were recovering in their baskets after minor operations.

'I'm Pippa Woodley,' I told her. 'I've come to see if there's any news of my pony.'

Her reassuring smile was answer enough.

'The mare's fine — none the worse for her trek through the storm,' she told me. 'In fact, my husband says that as things turned out the two-mile walk was the best treatment she could have had. It isn't always like that, of course. Quiet, warmth and a dose of medicine, or an injection, is the usual routine. However, it's vital that the pony shouldn't be allowed to roll and sometimes, in really severe cases, keeping on the move can do the trick.'

'Hurrah!' I cheered. 'When can I have her back?'

Mrs Corrin smiled at my eagerness. 'My husband said that if Magic shows no sign of developing a chill by this evening you can take her back to the Pony Farm. Telephone him around six o'clock.'

'May I see her now?' I asked.

'I don't see why not.'

Mrs Corrin led me to the stable yard where a familiar chestnut head with a white star between the eyes was looking over the half-door of a loose-box.

'Magic!' My knees felt suddenly wobbly as I ran over the cobbles to make much of her. Meanwhile, the vet's wife went indoors to answer the telephone.

My pony seemed glad to see me. She stretched her neck and thrust her head to my shoulder. Putting my hands around her muzzle I pressed my cheek against hers, suddenly overcome with emotion at the reunion.

Then, because, I suppose, of the hassle of Ruby leaving us in the lurch, Mrs Farley's second burglary and Magic's colic and recovery – I wept. Silly me! The tears flowed. How thankful I was that no one was there to see.

After a few minutes, I dried my eyes, blew my nose vigorously and felt ready to tackle anything that lay ahead.

10

An unwilling helper

Surprise! Surprise!

When we returned to the Pony Farm we found that, not only had Ruby and Kevin come back, but Ruby had actually prepared a super meal for us in the farmhouse kitchen.

It was as though she wanted to make amends for leaving Jane and me to cope by ourselves. She told us that the horse-box had broken down and that she and Kevin had to camp out in one of the caravans in a field near the garage while the vehicle was mended.

'But not to worry, petals. From now on Kev and I will be around all the time to help you,' she assured us as she served the meal of fried chicken, chips and fresh garden peas.

While Ruby was dishing up, Kevin was slumped over the *Racing News*.

'Now don't take any notice of Kevin,' Ruby said. 'He doesn't like to be interrupted when he's studying form. If he backs any more losers he'll blame you four for taking his mind off his reckoning.'

Delicious though the meal was, Kevin didn't even seem to notice what he was eating. With the racing paper propped against a beer can, he seemed lost amid the runners for the four-thirty.

'Right!' he said at last, his mouth full of blackcurrant cheesecake. 'I'll phone the bookie.'

To our amazement, instead of betting in the modest sums we had expected, Kevin told the bookmaker that he wanted to put thirty pounds each way on the two-thirty at Exeter, adding: 'And I'll have another thirty quid on Lively Lady in the three o'clock.'

'Kevin!' Ruby jumped up from the table. 'Have you gone mad? You usually limit your betting to three pounds a day.'

'So what?' He held her at arm's length as she tried to take the telephone from him. 'I've had a bit of a windfall – and now's my chance to speculate to accumulate.' Dodging Ruby he transferred the instrument to his other hand and quickly gave his final bet. 'Put me a tenner on Green Goblin in the four-thirty.' He slammed down the handset and turned to the door. 'I'm going to have an hour's kip in the cottage. Then I'll be watching the racing on the telly.'

'Charming!' Jane exclaimed. 'Why do you put up with him, Ruby?'

'I suppose I can't help myself.' Ruby looked wistfully out of the window as Kevin strode across the yard and added half under her breath: 'I'm in love with him – more fool me!'

We nodded in agreement. Then the boys took over the washing up as their way of thanking Ruby for the super lunch.

While they were busy, Jane and I went out with Darren to look at Bracken and Dandy in Little Paddock. The foal's limp had almost gone. Ruby's water-treatment with the hose had obviously worked. Jane called Dandy to us and I let him suck my fingers while she gently felt his hock.

'There's not much heat left and the swelling's going down.'

'I'm so glad.' I was relieved that Magic's accidental kick hadn't done any lasting harm to the foal.

Magic! I was longing to phone to see how she was and whether I'd be able to fetch her that evening, but the vet's wife had told me to ring at six o'clock and I didn't want to make a nuisance of myself before then.

To pass the time we went across the field to watch the other ponies. Queenie and Cobweb seemed to have settled down quite well, although the Exmoors did not yet seem fully to have accepted them as part of their small herd. The two newcomers stood, hock-high, amid the bracken at the far end of the field, nose to tail, flicking the flies away from each other, while Jane's Aunt's Exmoors dozed in a bunch beneath the oak trees on a little hillock above the dried-up bed of the stream.

'Are you two just going to *watch* the ponies all

afternoon?' Darren was soon impatient. 'I want a ride.'

'Very well,' Jane agreed. 'I suppose we can saddle Bumble.' She turned to me. 'Would you get some bread, Pippa, and see if you can catch Bumble while I fetch the tack?'

The elderly Exmoor was a poor substitute for my darling Magic but there was a furry friendliness about her and a readiness to please that I found endearing. Jane lifted Darren into the saddle and we took it in turns to lead him, walking and trotting round the field.

Tea-time came at last and Kevin was in an even worse mood, having lost his bets.

'The horses were all right.' He was unwilling to admit his lack of judgment. 'But the jockeys were a poor bunch. Two were half-asleep and the other must have been got at. He deliberately pulled the race so as to let the favourite win. It was obviously a put-up job.'

'Come off it, Kev.' Ruby handed him a cup of tea. 'Why don't you admit that you can't pick the winners? You've lost nearly a hundred pounds today and where did that money come from, I'd like to know? You wouldn't even lend me a fiver this morning towards my new shoes. It seems to me that you've got enough money when you want it for yourself but you've never got any for me when I ask you for a loan.'

Jane and I looked at each other. Was Ruby becoming disenchanted with her idol?

'Oh, shut up, Rube,' Kevin's handsome face clouded. 'Haven't I enough to put up with, without you giving me a hard time?' He pushed away his plate and got sulkily to his feet. 'I'm off! Expect me when you see me.'

Slamming the door behind him he strode across the yard to the horse-box.

'Just a minute, Kevin.' I ran after him. 'Wait for me.'

I scrambled into the passenger seat before he could stop me.

'Get out!' he challenged irritably. 'What do you think you're doing?'

'Please, Kevin,' I begged. 'Give me a lift to the vet's to see if Magic's ready to come back.'

Kevin glared at me and, for a moment, I thought he was going to push me out of the cab.

Then he grunted, 'It'll cost you a packet of fags.'

'Cheap at the price,' I said, blithe at the thought of having my pony back again. 'Thank you, Kevin.'

*   *   *   *

When we pulled up outside the surgery the vet was just crossing the yard. He stopped at the sound of the horse-box and came across to the cab and opened the door on Kevin's side.

'I'm glad Pippa's got transport.' He sized up Kevin. 'You look a handy fellow. Will you help me box the mare?'

Kevin's jaw dropped. He was about to refuse and drive on when I said quickly: 'Come on, Kev. Be a sport. I'll keep you in cigarettes for the rest of the week.'

Kevin backed the horse-box into the stable yard. As he climbed down from the cab he swept his gaze round the loose-boxes.

'Which of these nags is yours?'

There was really no need to ask. At the sound of our footsteps Magic gave a whinny and her head appeared over the half-door at the end.

'Don't hang about then,' Kevin said irritably. 'Get a halter on her.'

Meanwhile the vet went indoors to answer the telephone.

As I slipped the halter over my pony's ears, Kevin let down the ramp with a bang that made her flinch. Then he looked impatiently at me.

'For Pete's sake, isn't she ready yet?' Pushing past me he grabbed at Magic's halter. 'Come on now.' He gave the rope a jerk.

'Don't rush her,' I protested. 'She's been awfully ill and you're scaring her.'

'You're as bad as Ruby,' Kevin growled. 'You'd spoil any animal.' He flicked Magic's neck with the end of the halter rope. 'Get a move on.'

Trying to shove him aside I made a grab for the rope.

'Please let me lead her,' I begged. 'She *is* my pony.'

'You'll be all day.' Kevin tugged again and

Magic, scared now, dug in her toes and jibbed. 'Defy me, would you?' Kevin raised a hand to slap. I dragged at his sleeve.

'Oh, Kevin, grow up!' I exclaimed. 'Don't take it out on Magic just because you can't pick the winners.'

Kevin seemed deaf.

'Stop!' I pleaded. 'Oh, please, stop!'

11

Tantrums and toffee apples

Just then Mr Corrin, the vet, emerged from a side door of the house. 'What's going on here?'

'The pony's playing up,' Kevin retorted. 'I'm doing this girl a favour. But I can't be all day about it.'

'You'll box the pony all the sooner if you're more patient.' The vet put himself between Kevin and Magic. 'The mare knows you, Pippa. You lead her.'

'Come on, Magic,' I said firmly. 'You've been in horse-boxes before. There's no need to be scared.'

Meekly Magic let me lead her to the vehicle. Then, to my dismay, she refused to budge.

'Oh, don't be such a silly,' I chided. 'There's nothing to make a fuss about.'

Impatiently Kevin tried to snatch her halter. 'Give her to me. I'll soon make her move. You're too soft with her. What this pony needs is a firm hand.'

'Maybe, but not yours, young man.' The vet stepped in front of Kevin. He grasped Magic's halter in a no-nonsense way. Then he placed his other hand firmly on her chestnut rump. 'Now then, girl. Walk on.'

Magic let herself be half-pushed, half-pulled up the ramp. With her fore-feet on the floor of the box she laid back her ears and suddenly stopped.

'Strange!' said the vet. 'There must be something about this box that she doesn't like.'

'I know what it is,' I suddenly exclaimed.

About the back of the horse-box there hung a heavy odour of wet wool.

'Sheep!' I explained. 'There've been sheep in here and Magic can smell them. She doesn't like sheep. She was jostled once by Dave's father's flock. They'd been dipped and she got in the way when they stampeded.' Plucking a strand of wool from the side of the horse-box I turned to Kevin. 'You've had sheep in here.'

Kevin's features set into an angry frown. 'So what? It was a couple of days ago. I was doing a good turn to a mate. I gave his sheep a lift to market.' He glared at me. 'We don't want to be here all evening. Haven't you got a lump of sugar to sweeten the pony?'

'No, I haven't.' Then, miraculously, my eyes lit on a half-eaten toffee apple which had rolled among the straw. I pounced on it. 'You won't want this now,' I told Kevin. 'You must have dropped it. It's all dirty.' I picked off bits of straw and grit and held it out to the vet. 'Do you think it'll hurt Magic to give her this? She adores anything sweet.'

'There's no harm in *tempting* her with it,' said the

vet, 'but don't let her eat it. Just show it her to take her mind off the smell of the sheep.'

Magic fell for the ruse. Sniffing busily at the toffee apple she followed me into the box. Although I felt mean at not letting her have her reward, I was relieved when Kevin and the vet put up the ramp and I was bolted into the dim rankness of the unkempt horse-box with my beloved pony.

Magic didn't like being in there with the sheep smell, and I was glad Kevin had replaced the partitions for Ruby's ponies after his unlikely good turn run with the sheep.

Between the partition and the side of the horse-box there wasn't much room for Magic to move. Otherwise I'm sure she would have played up. As it was, she just stood trembling, ears back, shifting uneasily as the horse-box jolted round corners and sometimes suddenly braked.

Water seeped in as Kevin drove through the still-swollen ford and that made my pony even more uneasy. The vehicle jolted and swayed as Kevin tried to make up lost speed. If it hadn't been for the partition, Magic would have been thrown off her feet. It was all I could do, by hanging on to her head-collar and soothing her sweating neck, to prevent her from panicking.

'This isn't going to make you any easier to box in future,' I sighed, moving hastily out of the way as she shifted her weight and nearly brought down her fore-foot on my toes.

At last, thankfully, we pulled up at the Pony

Farm. The ramp was let down and Jane and Pete helped me lead Magic out.

Darren, curious as ever, appeared on the scene to pat Magic who suddenly swung round her head to try to lick a toffee apple that was clutched in the boy's grubby hand.

'More toffee apples!' I exclaimed, remembering the one in the horse-box. 'What a coincidence!'

'You naughty boy.' Jane snatched the sweetmeat from her brother. 'You must have sneaked into the cottage and taken another from Kevin's box.'

Darren burst into tears. 'He won't mind. He's got lots and lots.'

'Oh, very well then. But you must tell Kevin you've had it,' Jane relented and then looked at me. 'Kevin's secret vice! I suppose he bought a stock at Dunster Fair. Toffee apples at his age. What next?'

'I wonder,' I said meaningly. 'Yes, I wonder . . .'

12

Is Kevin really a baddie?

'The more I see of Kevin the less I like him.' I unburdened myself over supper in the farmhouse kitchen that evening. 'He's not a very good type, you know.'

Dave nodded. 'Well, he's not really horsy . . .'

Jane agreed. 'Despite the fact that, according to Ruby, he once worked in a circus.'

'He was probably only a tent-rigger,' said Pete. 'He may not have had anything to do with the animals.'

'Yes, but the horse-box belongs to him,' said Jane.

'Of course, he might have made a living transporting horses and doing a bit of dealing,' I suggested.

'Well, no one seems to know much about him,' said Jane. 'I believe he once lived in these parts. Ruby said his grandfather was cowman on this very farm. Kevin must have been quite young when his parents moved away because that accent of his is definitely Bristol.'

'He's the kind of mystery I can do without.' I

recalled how callous Kevin had been when we went to fetch Magic from the vet's. 'He scares me.'

'Then you'd better keep out of his way, twin,' advised Pete.

'Easier said than done.' I took a sip of cocoa before turning to Jane. 'He's a dead loss here, you know. We would manage better without him.'

'But not without Ruby,' Jane pointed out, helping herself to more cheese, 'and where Kevin goes, she'd go too.'

'So we've got to put up with him, I suppose,' I groaned.

'It may not be for long,' Dave added thoughtfully. He pushed back his chair. 'Oh, why don't we say what's at the back of all our minds?' He looked at us in turn. 'Kevin *could* be some sort of crook, just one step ahead of the police. You've only got to piece together the clues . . .'

'I like Kevin,' broke in Darren. 'He gives me toffee apples.'

'Toffee apples – yes, there's a "clue",' said Dave. 'Toffee apples stolen from Mrs Farley's.'

'A toffee apple in the horse-box,' added Jane.

'And another filched by Darren from Kevin's hoard,' said Dave.

'Kevin could be the one who broke into Mrs Farley's shop.' I sipped my cocoa. 'But I can't believe anything really bad of Ruby. Oh, I know she's silly, and infatuated with Kevin because he's big and handsome. But I don't think she's dishonest. She's got such a kind heart. Think how she's always adopting homeless ponies.'

'Perhaps Kevin broke into the shop while Ruby was buying her shoes,' said Jane.

'He'd have to be really bad to rob a widow like Mrs Farley,' observed Dave.

'Then there are the missing sheep,' I said slowly. 'When Kevin and I went to pick up Magic, the horse-box definitely smelled of sheep.'

Dave's eyebrows rose. 'You mean you think that Kevin stole the trials sheep?'

'I don't know,' I confessed. 'All I say is that the sheep were missing when the Hickson boys went to collect them from the farm and that Kevin recently carried sheep in his horse-box.'

'He could hardly lift a flock of sheep without Ruby knowing,' pointed out Jane.

'Not if she was there,' I admitted, 'but couldn't Kevin have pretended that the van broke down, bundled Ruby into a caravan park, met an accomplice and then gone back to pick up the sheep?'

'Could be.' Dave got up from the table. 'I'm going to telephone Sergeant Hickson and tell him what we suspect.'

'Wait a minute.' Dave paused while helping himself to a slice of fruit cake. 'The sergeant might think we're just a bunch of kids playing amateur detectives. Oh, I know the police always welcome information but suppose these clues are all *coincidences*.'

'What do you suggest we do then?' Pete asked.

'Keep our eyes and ears open,' said Dave. 'Then decide tomorrow.'

'And meanwhile,' I said, 'be on our guard because, you know, Kevin really is a menace.'

'Oi! Oi!' echoed a voice from the doorway and we all turned in shocked surprise to see Kevin standing right there.

I shivered. How long had he been in the passage? How much had he overheard?

'Dishing the dirt about me?' He moved to the window, blocking the light with his big frame. 'What am I supposed to have been up to?' He stared round at us. 'Well, come on. Say something. Otherwise I'll know you've been blackening my character.'

A silence fell. Then Darren jumped down from the table and ran to Kevin's side, looked up at him and said: 'Pippa says you're a men-ace!'

'Does she, by golly?' He glared at me and then stared at the others accusingly. 'No wonder you're all looking ashamed.' He threw a purple-wrapped packet on the table. 'Ruby sent you these chocolate biscuits. I hope they choke you!' He turned on his heel, glaring over his shoulder: 'And watch it, young Pippa. Just watch it!'

I shuddered as he slammed the door behind him. Yes, I was definitely frightened of Kevin.

'Phew!' Dave mopped the sweat from his brow. 'Now the cat is out of the bag!'

'I'm scared,' I admitted. 'That Kevin's a really nasty customer.' Across the table I met my twin's gaze. 'Do you think we ought to phone Mummy and Daddy, Pete? They'd know what to do.'

'All they'd say is to come home right away.' Pete's jaw set. 'No way! We must see this thing through. Besides, we don't want to go worrying Mum and Dad, nor Dave's parents, least of all now when they've got their hands full with summer visitors.'

*   *   *   *

The world looked better next morning as I craned out of the window to look for Magic in the pony field. August cobwebs sparkled on the rose leaves and heavy dew shimmered like a million diamonds on the grass.

I tried hard to forget about Kevin and his threatening ways as I saw my pony cropping the meadow. The Exmoors and Cobweb were still drowsing, but evidently Magic's stay in the vet's stable had made her appreciate fresh grass. She seemed not to want to waste a moment before grazing her fill.

As I watched I gazed at her, puzzled. Somehow my pony looked different. Then I realised why. Her chestnut legs ended in black socks. She was coated in mud up to her hocks!

'What's happened?' Jane joined me at the window.

'Magic looks as if she's been wading in mud.'

'She's probably been trying to follow the bed of

the stream in search of fresh water,' said Jane. 'The other ponies know what happened to the stream but Magic doesn't because she was at the vet's when they discovered the water had changed course.'

'I know,' I nodded. 'Just the same it's odd. The stream-bed dried so much yesterday with the wind and sun that I wouldn't have thought there was enough soggy mud to get Magic so black. Come on.' I collected my sponge-bag and tooth-mug. 'Let's get dressed. Then we can go down and see what she's been doing.'

Our footprints made tracks on the dew-wet meadow as we walked towards the ponies.

'What a state you're in, Magic.' I patted my pony's neck as she blew a greeting. 'I hope you didn't make another gap in the hedge when you were looking for the stream.'

The other ponies followed inquisitively as Jane and I inspected the boundaries. There was no sign of a break-out.

'Don't worry any more about it,' Jane said. 'Magic must have found a soft patch somewhere in the stream-bed. The mud will soon come off with a dandy brush. Look!' She pointed across the grass to the edge of a brackeny hollow. 'Is that a mushroom? They're early this year. Let's see if we can find enough for breakfast to give the boys a treat.'

We both filled our handkerchiefs with mushrooms and then Jane went indoors to fry them with bacon while I removed the mud from Magic's legs.

Before long a bark heralded Glen. Tail waving, he loped across the field to see what was afoot. He was followed a few minutes later by Dave and Pete. Still tousle-headed from sleep and in their dressing-gowns, they were on their way from their tent to the house to wash.

Putting the dandy brush on the tack-room shelf I was about to follow the boys to see if I could give Jane a hand in preparing the breakfast. I was stopped in my tracks by the sight of Darren, still in his pyjamas. His slippers and legs were soaked with dew as he wriggled through the field fence and came running across to me.

'Where have you been?' I scolded. 'I don't suppose Jane even knows you're up, let alone running round the field in your nightwear.'

Disarmingly Darren opened a muddy fist to show a button mushroom on his palm. 'You and Jane were looking for mushrooms. So I thought I'd help.'

'Where were you then?' I asked. 'I didn't see you in the field.'

Darren waved the mushroom vaguely in the direction of the stream-bed.

'That's not the only thing I found.' Transferring the mushroom to his left hand, he delved into his dressing-gown pocket and brought out a crinkly oblong of paper bearing the Queen's head and printed in brown ink.

'Look!' he crowed. 'Money! Lots of it! I'll buy you and Jane iced lollies when we go to town.'

I stared in disbelief at a ten-pound note! Then I held out my hand. 'Let's see, Darren.'

'No. It's mine.' Darren skipped out of reach. 'I found it.'

'Where did you find it?'

'Shan't tell.' Darren's mouth set. 'That's my secret!'

A big, dark shadow fell across the cobbles and I looked up to see Kevin towering over us.

'What's going on?' he demanded. 'Well, don't stand there like a dummy, Pippa. Say something!'

13

Where's Darren?

'Darren's found a ten-pound note.' I tried to keep my voice steady. 'But he won't say where.'

'It's mine,' Kevin said abruptly. 'I must have dropped it. Hand it over, Darren.'

'Shan't!' Darren looked sulky and began to run across the yard. 'Not even for toffee apples,' he called back over his shoulder.

At that moment Ruby emerged from the cottage. Darren dodged round her and taunted Kevin. 'You can't catch me.'

'Come back, you little wretch!' Kevin lunged after him but Ruby placed herself between him and the child.

'What's all this about?' she wanted to know.

'Oh, Darren's in trouble again.' I tried to make my tone steady. 'Somehow he seems to have got hold of a ten-pound note. Kevin says it's his.'

Ruby's lips seemed to tremble as she looked at her boyfriend. 'You said you hadn't got any money left when you'd settled up with the bookie last night.' She grabbed the note from Darren. 'I'll take charge of this.' She crammed it into the pocket of her blouse and then said to Kevin: 'Go inside. I want to have a word with you.'

Kevin glowered and hesitated. Then, to my surprise, he shrugged and followed Ruby inside. I heard the sudden burst of music from Ruby's transistor, probably turned on loud to drown their angry voices, and I felt suddenly unhappy.

Why, oh why, had Ruby had to bring Kevin with her to the Pony Farm to spoil such a perfect place?

*   *   *   *

Somehow the sunshine seemed to have gone from the morning. Over breakfast the others were making an effort to chatter cheerfully but I felt I couldn't, even when Jane suggested over the washing up that we might go for a ride.

'The vet said Magic wasn't to be ridden for a few days,' I pointed out.

'Yes, I know,' said Jane, 'but you can ride Cobweb or one of the Exmoors. Cheer up, Pippa.'

'I think I'd like to try Heather.' I turned to my brother. 'Which pony do you fancy?'

'None. Dave and I won't be riding this morning,' said Pete. 'We're going to be busy.'

'Oh! How?' I queried.

'We thought we'd give Glen a training session.' Dave spoke rather quickly. 'We don't want him to forget all that he's learnt.'

'Surely you don't intend to spend the whole

morning training Glen?' I looked squarely at Dave who dropped his gaze. 'You always say that after the first hour Glen tends to get stale.'

'Well, that's not the only thing we're going to do.' Pete looked round to make sure that neither Kevin nor Ruby were within hearing. 'Actually we're going to Abbot's Coombe to give another report to the police.'

'Another report!' gasped Jane. 'I thought we'd all decided not to say anything about Kevin until we were absolutely *sure*.'

'Well, Pete and I had second thoughts,' Dave confessed. 'So instead of going straight to the tent we went across the field to the phone box and reported to Sergeant Hickson. He told us not to tell our suspicions to anyone and to carry on normally. But we're to keep our eyes open and report anything else that might be suspicious.'

I blinked at him in amazement. 'Don't you think you were taking a lot on yourselves to phone the police without talking it over with Jane and me?'

'Well, when we were discussing it in the kitchen we hadn't quite made up our minds,' said Pete. 'Later, when Dave and I talked it over, we thought it might be best not to say anything to you two girls.'

'Oh, charming!' I exploded.

'We thought you might not be able to hide your feelings.' Dave looked apologetic. 'And we didn't want Kevin to tumble to the fact that we suspected him in case he did a bunk before Sergeant Hickson had time to complete his enquiries.'

'I see.' My tone was icy. 'In that case why are you telling us now?'

'Because we're going to Abbot's Coombe,' said Dave, 'and we wanted you two girls to be on your guard in case Kevin turns nasty.' He looked at us seriously. 'If I were you, I'd keep well out of his way.'

'Very well. We'll definitely go for a ride,' said Jane quickly. 'Pippa can take Heather. I'll ride Cobweb and lead Bumble with Darren.'

*　*　*　*

During the ride Jane had plenty to occupy her mind, instructing Darren to sit up straight and keep his heels down and hold his reins properly. I tried to push any thought of Kevin to the back of my mind and to enjoy the ride.

It was a lovely summer's morning and the bees were humming above the bell heather as we took the winding lane that led over the shoulder of the moor.

With Darren on the leading rein, Jane didn't want to go faster than a trot. When we reached Tankerly crossroads, however, she suggested that I should carry on for a longer ride over the moor, making my own way back while she and Darren followed the road to the Pony Farm.

'It'll give you a chance to have a gallop. Meanwhile I'll be back at the farm getting lunch.'

'But what about Kevin?' I objected. 'I don't think the boys would want me to let you go back on your own.'

'Ruby will be there,' pointed out Jane, 'and I don't suppose it will be long before Dave and Pete get back. Anyway, once I've unsaddled the ponies I shall go in to the house and lock the door. Go on!' She gave Heather's quarters a light slap. 'Enjoy the chance of a good canter.'

*   *   *   *

To my relief, the horse-box was not in the stable yard when I returned and there was no sign of Kevin around the cottage. Perhaps he'd done what the boys had feared and decided to make a break for it. I hoped so because I dreaded encountering him again. I told myself that Sergeant Hickson and the police patrols would soon catch up with him wherever he'd gone.

'That you, Pippa?' Jane's head looked out of the kitchen window. 'I hope you don't mind sausages . . . There's no sign of the boys yet so I thought I'd cook something that would be none the worse for having to be kept hot.'

'Sausages are fine by me,' I assured her as I slid from the saddle and pulled Heather's reins over her head. 'But where are Kevin and Ruby and the horse-box? Has Kevin really done a bolt?'

Jane's eyes flickered in anxiety.

'Well, if he has, he's taken Ruby with him.'

Just then Heather started to shake her head, impatient to be free of her tack and to join her companions in the field.

'I'll unsaddle Heather and turn her out,' I called to Jane.

'All right. Come straight back. Lunch is almost ready. Dave and Pete can have theirs later. Give Darren a shout. He'll be in the orchard looking for windfalls for the ponies.'

There was no trace of Darren in the orchard, however, nor in Little Paddock where Bracken was suckling her foal.

There'd been no sign of him either in the home field. Pehaps he was in one of the outbuildings. I looked into the tack room and food store. I even went to Firebird's loose-box and the barn.

'Darren!' I shouted. '*Darren*! Where are you?'

At that moment Pete and Dave came back with Glen.

'Did you see anything of Darren as you came up the lane?' I asked the boys.

My brother shook his head. 'I expect he'll turn up when he's hungry.' He sniffed the aroma of fried sausages. 'Bangers and mash! Just the job.'

Darren didn't show up over lunch. By the time we'd reached the apple-pie stage we were getting really worried.

'Where on earth can he have got to?' Jane puzzled. 'It's not like Darren to miss a meal.'

'I'll take my bike and have a scout round the lanes.' Pete swallowed a last spoonful of pie and pushed back his chair.

'Good idea,' Jane said gratefully, 'and I suppose I'd better give Mrs Farley a ring. It's just possible Darren might have tried to walk to her shop in search of ice-cream and toffee apples.'

Mrs Farley told us that Darren hadn't been to the shop.

'I wonder where he could have gone?' Dave looked thoughtful as he tried to put himself into a small boy's frame of mind. 'Could he have somehow found a way into the cottage to look for Kevin's toffee apples and any more ten-pound notes? He might just have got himself shut in. We'd better organise a search.'

The cottage, however, was securely locked and all the windows shut. There was no sign of Darren there. We re-visited all the outbuildings, yelling ourselves hoarse. Then Jane decided there was nothing else for it but to saddle three of the Exmoors for Dave, me and herself and to search the neighbouring fields and moorland, while Pete concentrated on the roads.

While Dave and Jane set off for the moor, I decided to explore nearer home.

I was riding Bumble and, as I trotted down the lane, Magic came to the hedge of the home field to whinny protestingly. She had already made a fuss when we caught the Exmoors as if she didn't want to be left behind again. Obviously she was feeling fit and frisky. Anxious though I was about Darren I couldn't help feeling relieved. At the same time I noticed that my pony had once again got herself caked in mud to the hocks. I glanced, puzzled, at the bed of the former stream.

It now looked as if the sun had baked it quite dry. Was water still left in one of the deeper gullies or had Magic found some other hidden source of water?

At that moment my pony stretched her neck over the hedge in further protest and snorted at the normally placid Bumble.

Sensing Magic's jealousy the Exmoor shied. Her rather worn girth slipped, taking the saddle with it.

I suddenly found myself upside-down!

14

Darren's discovery

I landed with a bump on my shoulders and just managed to roll out of the way of Bumble's hooves as she cantered down the lane.

'Oh, dear!' I groaned. 'This isn't getting us any nearer to finding Darren.'

I picked myself up and set off after Bumble who had disappeared round the bend.

After rounding a couple more bends I found the pony by the lane-side, her mealy muzzle calming cropping the grass. Thankful for her quiet nature, I remounted and scanned the area. I paid particular attention to the new course of the stream. Like all small boys, Darren was fascinated by water. So, disappointed by the drying up of the brook, he might well have made his way to the culvert, thinking that where the stream ran through the woodland he might be able to build a dam or to fish.

There was no sign of him so I rode up the hill. I went as far as I thought it possible for such a small boy to have wandered and then I started to zig-zag across my route, looking into every hollow in the bracken and investigating every clump of hawthorn and gorse, searching the coverts into which Darren might have crawled and perhaps gone to sleep.

I shouted his name until I was hoarse. Then, as I rode back towards the Pony Farm, I heard my twin's voice from the lane also shouting, 'Darren!'

Jane and Dave were already back at the stable yard and Glen bounded towards us running from Pete and his bicycle to me and Bumble as we arrived.

'It's almost four o'clock.' Jane was looking worried. 'I know it's quite a long time to nightfall but I think we ought to call the police.'

She went into the house to telephone and the rest of us unsaddled the ponies and continued with our search on foot.

As I visited the fallow field for the third time Magic called to me over the hedge. I crossed to speak to her and noticed again her mud-caked legs. As I scrambled over the gate to join her she trotted off to the far end of the field as though to let me know she wasn't yet ready to be caught.

I stood still, watching her. She was now trace-high in the bracken that covered the far end of the field. The Exmoors were at the other end, clustered near Pete who was searching the hedgerow. No doubt they were hoping for food.

Magic, however, took no notice of Pete. She was walking purposefully on her way through the bracken. Was she returning to some hidden spring? Scorning to drink tap-water from the trough, her Arab ancestry might have enabled her to scent water for herself and discover her own supply. Might she not even now be on her way to drink? Wasn't it just possible that Darren had followed Magic to her secret water source and had some mishap?

'Pete!' I broke into a run. 'Come quickly. We must follow Magic.'

'Coming!' My brother sped across the grass dropping to a cautious walk as he reached the bracken. 'Steady, Pippa.' He signalled me to slow down. 'It's no use panicking the mare. Don't let her realise we're following or she may change her mind about going to drink.'

'How did you know she was going to water?' I looked at my twin in puzzlement.

'I suppose I must have beamed into your thought-waves, Pippa,' my twin admitted. 'It's happened before. Telepathy.'

'But not lately,' I said as we waded through the bracken in Magic's wake. 'Just recently you've had more time for Dave and Glen than for Magic and me.'

'I suppose so,' Pete agreed, 'but although we're twins you have to understand, Pippa, I have to do boys' things sometimes.'

Magic was disappearing into a hollow amid the bracken and now there were 'sucking' noises as she lifted her feet.

'Boggy ground,' I said to Pete. 'There must be a

spring. Now Magic's drinking. Do you think Darren could have followed her here and perhaps twisted his ankle and fallen?'

'Or just curled up and gone to sleep,' said Pete. 'After all, it's a hot day. Listen!' He turned his head. 'Did you hear that? It sounded like a child's voice, only muffled.' He bent to shout. 'Darren! Where are you?'

'Down here . . . Get me out! It's dark and nasty.' The boy's voice was clearer now. 'I fell.'

I started to run but Pete caught my arm. 'Careful, Pippa. There must be an old well somewhere in the bracken.'

Pete gingerly edged forward and caught a shoe against the displaced wooden cover of a well.

Parting the overgrowing fronds we peered into blackness. It was impossible to judge the depth of the well but Darren's voice did not seem to come from too far down. Perhaps he was on a ledge.

As we peered over the rim I happened to dislodge a crumbly piece of mortar which passed the child to fall with a hollow plop into the water below.

'Have you hurt yourself, Darren?' I called urgently.

'Only my knee.' Darren was trying to be brave. 'I bumped it but it doesn't hurt much. I've been down here for hours. It's horrid and slimy.'

'Well, hang on a bit longer, there's a good chap,' Pete encouraged. 'Pippa will stay and talk to you. I'm going to get help.'

Watching Pete bounding away through the bracken towards the farm I caught the glint of sunlight winking on metal as a police car swept into the yard and, to my surprise, drove straight into the barn.

Strange, I thought! Why were the police trying to keep the squad car out of sight? In case Kevin should come back in the horse-box, see it and drive off again?

Then, from the barn, came Sergeant Hickson, a young constable and Mrs Farley!

Help had indeed arrived. I beckoned and shouted to the grown-ups and soon we were all grouped near the well.

'It won't be long now, Darren,' the sergeant called. 'We'll soon have you out.'

'Whatever made you wander off on your own and get into such a pickle?' shouted Mrs Farley.

'I followed Magic,' answered Darren's plaintive voice. 'I wanted to see how she got so muddy. I thought perhaps there was still some of the stream left somewhere and I could make a dam.'

'Magic didn't come to the well,' I pointed out. 'She found water in the boggy ground.'

'I know,' said Darren echoed. 'But I found some more money and I thought there might be still more down here.' A scrabbling noise sounded from inside the well. 'There is something down here – sort of boxes and a bag. I can't open them and I can't feel what's inside!'

15

Three cheers for Magic

'Look out, Darren,' Sergeant Hickson shouted over the edge of the well. 'We're lowering a ladder.'

When the ladder was in position the sergeant knotted a rope round Pete's waist.

'You'll be lighter than me, lad,' he said. 'So down you go.'

While Pete was descending, Sergeant Hickson and P.C. Bolton stood by the ladder, holding it firm.

'I've got Darren now,' came Pete's voice a few minutes later. 'I'm going to lift him onto the ladder. If I can edge him up a few more rungs you might be able to lean over and grab him.'

'Jane! Pippa!' Sergeant Hickson said. 'Come and help me hold on to the ladder. Frank!' He turned to P.C. Bolton. 'Lean over as far as you can, ready to take the child. Tessa!' He turned to Mrs Farley. 'Grab the constable's ankles.'

There came an alarming plop as more of the brickwork fell away. The base of the ladder still stayed firm, however, and a few moments later Pete was able to edge Darren up rung by rung.

P.C. Bolton lay over the rim of the well with Mrs Farley and Dave clinging to his ankles.

Next minute the young constable gripped Darren by the wrists and pulled him to safety. A few moments later Pete's face appeared at the top of the ladder and soon he, too, was clear of the well.

'Well done, lad,' Sergeant Hickson said warmly.

Meanwhile Pete was delving into his pocket to produce a folded plastic bag. 'There was a lot of stuff down there,' he told the sergeant. 'So I've brought up a sample.'

Sergeant Hickson unrolled the container to reveal some money in one-, five- and ten-pound notes.

'Good lad!' said the sergeant. 'Now we are getting some evidence.' He looked across at Mrs Farley. 'This could be the money from your till, Tessa.'

'There's a lot more stuff down there,' Pete told the sergeant excitedly. I could feel cartons — perhaps cigarettes.'

Sergeant Hickson nodded to the young constable. 'Wait here, Frank, and keep guard. I'll go back and put out an all-stations call to intercept the horse-box.'

However, when we reached the crest of the hillock beyond the stream-bed, we saw, to our surprise, that Kevin's horse-box was standing in front of the farmhouse. So he had come back. Why? To collect his loot?

'Right!' Sergeant Hickson turned to Pete.

'Double back and tell P.C. Bolton we want him.'

We had only gone a few yards when Jane suddenly pointed to a slim figure creeping round the stable buildings.

'Micky Smith!' she gasped. 'What's he doing here?'

'He's probably heard on the grapevine that his sister's running around with a rotter and he's hared over to sort it out,' said Dave.

'That's it!' I answered. 'And now perhaps he's trying to stop Kevin making a get-away.'

We watched as the Pony Farm's former stable-lad bent to fiddle with the front near-side wheel of the horse-box and then doubled out of sight, probably to remove the valve at the other side.

'Just the ticket!' Sergeant Hickson chuckled before looking warningly round at us. 'There may be a bit of trouble over this. Keep back. The constable and I will cope if there's any rough stuff.'

At that moment Kevin ran from the cottage. He glanced across the fields, saw Sergeant Hickson and the rest of us and made a dash towards the horse-box just as Micky was about to let down the last of the tyres.

With an angry shout, Kevin launched himself towards Micky who dodged his flailing fists and fled into the low shed which served as a tack room.

Kevin was on Micky's heels but, blinded by temper, he forgot the low lintel of the doorway. He caught his head against the top. Thwack! The impact knocked him off his balance and, half-stunned, he sank to the ground.

Just then Ruby ran from the cottage.

'Kevin, you're hurt!' She knelt beside him.

'Don't waste your pity on him,' Sergeant Hickson advised as he breathlessly reached her side. 'The knacker at Dunster gave us a statement to the effect that Kevin had arranged to sell your own three ponies to him for dog-meat. Kevin was going to deliver them later today.'

'Cobweb, Firebird and Queenie!' Ruby gasped. She rounded on her boyfriend. 'How could you, Kevin? You pretended you loved me. Oh, I can see it all now. You've just been using me for your own ends, as a cover for your greedy thieving.'

Kevin sat up, groggily. 'Shut up, Ruby! Do you want to land me in jail? I do love you, and I'll marry you if only you'll hold your tongue.'

'Marry her!' Sergeant Hickson's tone was scornful. 'According to the Bristol police you're already married, with a couple of kids.'

'You rotter!' In her disgust Ruby slapped Kevin across the face. This seemed to revive him and he staggered to his feet in time for P.C. Bolton to reach his side and click on the handcuffs.

'We've already arrested your accomplice, and now we're taking you to the Police Station where you'll be charged with sheep-stealing, and breaking and entering,' the sergeant informed Kevin. 'I think you'll be out of circulation for quite a time, my lad.'

'Good riddance!' said Ruby indignantly. Then,

to everyone's consternation, she burst into tears.

'There, there.' Mrs Farley put her arms round her. 'You've had a shock. But it isn't the end of the world, my dear. Someday you'll know what true love really is.' She paused before adding: 'Time will heal, Ruby. That's something I've had to learn.'

'I've learned something, too,' suddenly confessed Micky. 'A fellow doesn't get on in the world by letting people down. It was the worst thing I ever did to walk out of here and go to that racing stable, Jane.'

'So it didn't work out, Micky?' Jane was sympathetic.

'I'd never have been offered an apprenticeship,' Micky said. 'As the other lads soon told me, I'm not small enough to make a jockey.'

'Then why did the trainer offer you the job?' asked Pete.

'Because two of the other stable-lads had left and the boss couldn't get anyone else at short notice,' Micky said bitterly. 'I was only a stop-gap.'

'And you seemed so happy,' I said, recalling the cheerful letter he had written.

'It was only wishful thinking.' Micky's eyes dropped and he kicked at a piece of straw. 'Now I'm out of a job.'

*　　*　　*　　*

'Look! Magic wants to join the party!'

In mischief as usual, my pony had somehow managed to nose up the catch of the field gate. Now she had come to look through the window of the farmhouse sitting-room where, a week later, we were celebrating Jane's Aunt's return from her cruise.

Looking sun-tanned and happy, Auntie Sue was helping Ruby and Mrs Farley to lay out plates of sausage rolls, sandwiches, chocolate cake, jugs of iced orangeade and bowls of strawberries and cream.

By the music-centre Jane and Micky were sorting through a pile of records. Jane's Aunt tried not to flinch as the beat of Pink Confusion blared through the room. 'Oh, I am enjoying myself,' she declared firmly. 'It's so nice to have some young life about the place.'

'Including Magic?' I laughed as Sergeant Hickson opened the window for Darren to give a lump of sugar to my pony.

Across the room the Hickson boys started to dance, calling to Jane and me to join them.

'This is going to be the best rave-up yet, Pippa,' Jimmy announced close to my ear.

Then, all talk drowned by the music, Dave and Pete took to the floor – Pete making a threesome with George and Jane, and Dave joining in with Jimmy and me. Through the window Magic's head seemed to be nodding in time with the beat.

Dear Magic! I thought. There she was, naughty

as usual, but I had to forgive her this time. This was a time for happiness. Across the room a diamond-cluster engagement ring sparkled on Mrs Farley's left hand. Yes, she and Sergeant Hickson were getting married in the autumn.

And Micky? He'd got his old job back and he and Ruby were living in the cottage and helping with the ponies.

'Enjoying yourself, Pippa?' Micky yelled above the music.

'Yes, and so is Ruby.' I nodded towards the open window where Ruby had doubled up with laughter as Magic stretched her head through to filch a sausage roll from the plate she was holding.

'Three cheers for Magic!' called Darren as the disc ended and my pony whinnied for more party fare.

'And for Glen – for coming in second in the trials,' added Dave.

'Hip! Hip!' shouted Dave.

'Woof! Woof!' barked Glen.

'Hurrah!' We all cheered. 'Hurrah! Hurrah!'

You may also like to read the other books in this series:

PONY-TREKKERS, GO HOME

JUDITH BERRISFORD

Pony-mad Pippa was overjoyed to be spending three weeks' holiday at her Aunt Carol's pony-trekking centre in Scotland. Even her brother Pete was converted when Lord Glencairn allowed the twins to ride his own expensive ponies.

But there was something that puzzled Pippa about Lord Glencairn's stables. Why were famous show jumpers lodged there – especially Ballantrae? And was there an explanation for the villagers' hostile attitude towards the trekking centre? Sworn to secrecy by Lord Glencairn himself, Pippa and Pete were left to try and solve the mystery themselves . . .

The first book in the Pippa Pony series

KNIGHT BOOKS

SABOTAGE AT STABLEWAYS

JUDITH BERRISFORD

A cut stirrup-leather was one of several puzzling disasters that had occurred at Stableways, where Pippa worked as a helper. Obviously someone was trying to discredit the riding establishment. But who? And why?

As the Boxheath Trials drew near, Pippa and her twin brother Pete worked like mad at their own jumping, while the happenings at the stables became increasingly sinister. Sabotage was one thing, but deliberate attempts to hurt the ponies were even more distressing to Pippa. Also, she seriously began to wonder if Stableways would be able to muster a team to enter at the Trials . . .

The second book in the Pippa Pony series

KNIGHT BOOKS

PIPPA'S MYSTERY HORSE

JUDITH BERRISFORD

On holiday in the West Country, Pippa and her twin brother Pete rescued a shipwrecked horse. He was in such a miserable state that they feared what the vet's verdict might be, and then there were the insurers to deal with . . .

Pippa was overjoyed when the horse was given a second chance — because he was a rare and valuable appaloosa — and with loving care she restored the animal to health.

Pippa knew that the appaloosa should be returned to his rightful owner but was worried by his mysterious past. The horse had been carefully trained, but also very cruelly treated. Surely not by the same person? How would she be able to find and identify the *real* owner?

The third book in the Pippa Pony Series

KNIGHT BOOKS

More Pippa Pony stories
from Knight Books

JUDITH BERRISFORD

☐ 26599 X   Pony-Trekkers, Go Home   85p
☐ 26812 3   Sabotage At Stableways   95p
☐ 26811 5   Pippa's Mystery Horse   £1.25

All these books are available at your local bookshop or newsagent, or can be ordered direct from the publisher. Just tick the titles you want and fill in the form below.

Prices and availability subject to change without notice.

KNIGHT BOOKS, P.O. Box 11, Falmouth, Cornwall.

Please send cheque or postal order, and allow the following for postage and packing:
U.K. – 45p for one book, plus 20p for the second book, and 14p for each additional book ordered up to a £1.63 maximum.

B.F.P.O. and EIRE – 45p for the first book, plus 20p for the second book, and 14p per copy for the next 7 books, 8p per book thereafter.

OTHER OVERSEAS CUSTOMERS – 75p for the first book, plus 21p per copy for each additional book.

Name..

Address..

....